LAST TRAIN TO MURDER
AND OTHER STORIES

By Rick L. Phillips, Laura, Nicole, Christopher Brockow and Steven Thompson

This book is dedicated to Jesus Christ my Lord and Saviour. To the Davy Jones Equine Memorial Fund and to the Monkees, Davy, Micky, Mike and Peter for all the happy moments they gave me and others in comedy and music.

OTHER BOOKS BY THE AUTHORS

BY RICK L. PHILLIPS

DINKY THE ELF

IT'S THAT TIME AGAIN VOLUME 3 (SHORT STORY TITLED "WAR BETWEEN TWO WORLDS")

PROJECT: HERO

WITH GREAT POWER

By CHRISTOPHER BROCKOW

TRANSITION

The Davy I Remember

By Laura Nicole © 2013

The Davy I remember is the first time I saw him on TV. 1986 I was only 4 but I saw those stars in his eyes and so the crush began. That same year I realized that he was older but I still had a crush on him. The first video I saw was "That was then, This is now". Still crushing on the man, even at a young age. The year was 2001, and I was about to see The Monkees for the first time. I was 19 years old. I couldn't have been acting more like a squealing little girl. I was BEYOND excited about seeing them. Especially Davy. He was as cute as ever. He went through the crowd handing out roses. Unfortunately, I didn't get one. But seeing him doing what he does best was priceless. They put on a fantastic show. Skip to exactly 10 years later, almost to the day I saw them the first time in concert. June 2011 they announced their 45th anniversary tour. I once again got to see one of my favorite bands rock the stage. Sadly that would be the last time I would see Davy. You see for me, it's not just one look or decade. It's was anytime I saw his face, it brought a smile to mine. I adore and love Davy. Have been for 27 years and will for the rest of my life. Same goes for the rest Micky, Mike, & Peter. They were my first band that I got into and have brought a lot of happiness to my life. Thanks to them and Facebook I have met some really groovy people that I call Friends. Finally after all these years I have people to share my "obsession".

Last Train to Murder
By Rick L. Phillips © 2011

Chapter 1

The year was 1967 and believe me there was a lot going on in that year. The Vietnam War was still going on. "Happenings" were…well happening all over and setting the stage for the summer of Love. Clint Eastwood's movie "A Fistful of Dollars" was released in the USA. Apollo 1 failed and caught fire on the launching pad. For me 1967 was the year I, Joshua Adams, graduated college. I longed for action and adventure. I was one of the few in my high school that hoped to be drafted. That could get me the action and adventure that I craved. A few weeks after high school in 1963, before I could enlist, I got my draft notice. On the way to the draft board I was in a car accident. I was in bad shape and my rib cage punctured one of my lungs. It had to be removed. After I got out of the hospital I still went to the draft board hoping I could get in the Army. No such luck. Thanks to only having one lung they wouldn't take me and labeled me 4F. I still wanted my share of action and adventure but no matter where I tired they wouldn't take me seriously with only having one lung. It was my Mother who suggested I become a reporter. I always did like to write and I was on my school paper, so I entered college as Journalism major. In 1967 I graduated with hopes of becoming a top crime reporter. My path to becoming a reporter didn't come about in the usual way. This is my story.

You never know where your big break is going to come from. I'm 22 years old and a journalism school graduate. I was in the top 10 of my class and had a part-time job at the Times but it wasn't much more than just emptying wastebaskets. When I graduated the part-time job ended too. I expected that they would offer me a full-time position. They always told me how well I was doing, so I was totally surprised when all I got was a card signed by the staff wishing me luck. I sent samples of my writings to all the major newspapers and magazines. They all said the samples showed talent but that I still needed seasoning to be a crime reporter. Reading between the lines they were really saying that I was too young with not enough experience. So when I got the offer to be a writer for the new teen magazine, The Fab Tab, I took it. Hey you have to pay the bills. To my surprise my editor asked that I cover the summer tour of The Monkees.

"I've watched the show sometimes," I said. "It's funny and the songs are pretty good but they're just actors aren't they?"

My editor looked up at me. "Boy you must have really had your head buried in the books. They're actors but they have been putting on concerts sometimes too. Now they're doing a summer tour and you have been cleared to cover it for The Fab Tab."

"When do I meet them?"

"Their show wrapped up for the season not long ago. So your meeting is scheduled tomorrow morning at their NBC offices at 9am."

With that I left the office. I stopped to get something to drink and picked up an evening paper. The front page story was how local business man and investor, Paul White, was found shot to death in his apartment. There were no witnesses and no weapon found. He was only found when the doorman went to deliver a package. After that I made a few calls to find out more about the Monkees. Then I made some possible questions to ask them. All that time, I thought this had to be the worst assignment any budding crime reporter could have. I would soon find out how wrong I was.

The next morning at 8:50 am I was driving through the entrance to NBC studios. It took me almost ten minutes to find a parking spot that wasn't already taken or marked for some studio executive. Just as my watch showed 9am I entered the outer office of Raybert Productions, the producer s of the TV show "The Monkees." A pretty red head young woman in a yellow dress sat at the desk facing the door. I quickly stepped up to her desk.

"Josh Adams for the Fab Tab." I said. "I'm here to do a story on The Monkees."

She looked at the appointment book. Then without even looking up she said, "You're late!" She then proceeded to go about her work.

"But I was told it was for 9am."

Without saying a word she raised her right arm and with her pencil in hand she pointed to the clock on the wall behind her. It said the time was 9:01am.

"I'm only a minute late. I had a hard time finding a parking place. Can you see if they'll still see me?"

She gave me a stern look as she raised her head up from her paperwork. Then she pleasantly smiled. As the cold stern look melted, her smile radiated warmth as she looked at me.

"I'm sorry. This time of year is hard as we are winding down for the summer. I was hoping to have been done by yesterday so I could leave on vacation with some friends today. If I get my work done early I can meet them at noon to take off. My name is Judy. "She held out her hand to me.

As I shook her hand I had to ask her a question. "Going anyplace interesting?"

"Living in sunny LA we thought of going someplace cooler. We decided to go camping in Canada and then come back home for some horseback riding that Davy bought for me."

"You're not exactly dressed for camping."

"I know I'll have to make a quick stop at my apartment to change. I'll see if they can see you now."

I looked at some pictures on the wall as she called to them on the intercom. Almost all of the pictures were of the Monkees. One was in black and white with three of them with their instruments and one was hanging by his knees from a pole above them. Another was in color of the four of them standing around a barber pole.

"Mr. Schneider and Mr. Rafelson will see you now, "said Judy.

She opened the office door and ushered me into the room. Inside the room were two desk and each had a producer seated behind it. At the desk to the left one producer was seated wearing reading glasses and typing away. He barely noticed me when I entered. On my right behind the other desk was a man leaning back in his chair with his feet on the desk and crossed at the ankles. He too was wearing glasses but it was a dark pair of sunglasses. I thought it was odd to see him wearing them inside. To my surprise the four stars of the show were also in attendance. Davy Jones was sitting on the corner of the desk of the man with the sunglasses. Seated next to him in a chair was Micky Dolenz. He was wearing a short sleeved shirt with stripes, dress pants and Beatle boots. Standing in the corner was Peter Tork who had on a short sleeved white shirt and pants with his belt buckled on the side. Mike Nesmith was seated next to the typing producers' desk. He was dressed in a tan business suit and had dark sunglasses like the other producer but his were in the breast pocket of his suit.

"So you're Josh Adams from the Fab Tab!" said the producer with the sunglasses. "I'm Bob Rafelson. The industrious typist over there is my partner Bert Schneider and I'm sure you know the rest of these gentlemen."

"Pleased to meet you," I said as I started to shake all of their hands.

Rafelson motioned towards an empty chair.

"Take a seat."

I grabbed the seat and said, "Where shall I take it?"

"Very funny, maybe we should hire you to be the fifth Monkee."

I sat down. Schneider quit typing and turned to face me. Rafelson took his feet off the desk and sat up. All eyes were on me. I knew this would be a serious meeting. Schneider was the first to speak.

"The boys have been taking a beating in the news lately. The Fab Tab is a new magazine and from what we have been told you are a new writer. With no track record for either we would like to know what direction you plan to take with this article."

"Just a straight day by day occurrence of what happens to them."

"So none of this about how they don't play their own instruments?"

"I've been in school studying to be a crime reporter. I haven't read much of the entertainment news."

Rafelson seemed to sit back with more ease.

"Well maybe a fresh look will be good for a change."

I thought of asking if they didn't play their instruments but realized that would hurt my little interview here. I also realized that they had to or they couldn't go on tour and play concerts.

"Well there is a bit of a change since we last talked to your editor."

"What kind of change?"

That is when Nesmith joined the conversation.

"Mr. Adams…"
"Call me Josh."

"Josh, just before you got here we were told that some of our concerts had to be postponed. Not an easy thing for us as it'll be hard to make them up with our tight schedule. But a network executive called Bob and was planning an affiliate's meeting. The majority share holder wants it held in his hometown where he grew up. His grandson is also going to be there and since it's his birthday he asked us to play. We don't normally do birthday parties but the amount he was paying made up for the concerts."

Davy looked at me and said, "So instead of letting us take some vacation time Bob said yes to the party for the Grandson and TV personalities."

"Personalities? Are there going to be other celebrities there?"

"Yeah but we don't have a list yet. It's probably a safe bet they'll all be from the network." Said Dolenz.

"But those guys aren't playing music like we are right?" Asked Tork.

The others looked at him with disgust and together said, "No Peter."

"Are we getting paid to play?"

They turned to him again with the same look. "Yes Peter."

"That's great but I still would have played for free."

I looked at Rafelson. "He's right this is great. Where do we go and when will we be leaving?"

"Well its short notice I know but you all leave tonight. You'll be heading to Clarksville, Indiana."

"Does Clarksville even have an airport?"

"They have a train station. The guy owns a railroad. So you'll be riding the rails there."

Dolenz turned and looked at me. He then acted like he was taking a cigar from his mouth and in his best imitation of a big Hollywood producer said, "Yes baby! We'll be taking the last train to Clarksville."

Chapter 2

It's after 11pm and I'm at the train station getting ready to board the train. Just like Dolenz said this is the last train to Clarksville. It departs at 11:35 pm. I spent most of the day packing and calling friends and family to tell them I was going to be away for awhile.

I saw Rafelson, Schneider and the Monkees on the platform waiting next to the train. As I approached them I started to wonder why there wasn't a crowd of teenage girls mobbing them. Then I noticed that most of the crowd was made of TV stars. I could understand why they wouldn't mob them. They probably saw them at the studios a lot and thought of them as co-workers. I suppose the few teens that were there were part of the celebrities' families and use to seeing famous people.

"Hi guys!"

They turned to see me and all said hello.

"I see there are a lot of people here for this late hour."

"Well most of these people are here for the trip to the party in Indiana." said Rafelson.

"So you and Mr. Schneider are coming along too Mr. Rafelson?"

"No," said Schneider. "We're just here to see the guys off. We're leaving a few days later at the airport. But like you said earlier we found out that Clarksville doesn't have an airport. From there we have almost an hour cab ride. You five will probably have a better trip then we will."

Rafelson looked at me. "Also, if we can call you Josh then you can call me Bob and I don't think he would mind if you call him Bert."

"Ok!"

We talked for awhile about the impending trip when I noticed a very pretty blonde in the background. Mike noticed and had to ask.

"What are you looking at buddy?"

"That blonde! She's beautiful! Do you know who she is?"

By that time the others were looking in that direction.

"Yeah that's Samantha Strong. She's on that new spy show I think it's called Espionage. She's a great girl," said Micky.

"I watch that show every week. She looks different in person. Actually she looks prettier."

Davy looked at her. She saw him and waved. He waved back.

Peter looked at Davy and smiled and said, "He's always trying to get her on a date. So far she's always said no."

"Peter you know what an actor's schedule is like? With both of us on TV shows and add in our music studio sessions and concerts we just can't find the time."

"Well I'm not an actor," I said. "If she wants to go with me I'm sure I can work my schedule around hers."

"Really now." said Davy.

I suddenly realized that, without meaning to, I had challenged him.

"She probably would rather go with you Davy."

"Don't back down now mate. It's a long train ride. We'll see who gets the girl in the end."

Suddenly there was the conductor leaning out of the train.

"All aboard!" He shouted.

We all gathered our suitcases and belongings and started to board. Bob and Bert were saying goodbye to us all. Peter was the first to turn and head toward the train when a man was running toward the train and Peter bumped into him. They both fell to the ground and the suitcases fell open. Both got to their feet and dusted themselves off. The man called Peter every name he could think of even though it really wasn't Peter's fault. Peter quickly put his hand out to shake the other man's hand. As he did he said he was sorry. The man misunderstood his quick move and stepped back. As he did he tripped over his suitcase again and fell to the ground again. By this time a group of railroad employees had gathered around them.

"Did you see that?" he said.

"Yes Mr. Pitts!" said the railroad workers as if it had been rehearsed.

"Just because he's on TV he thinks he can get violent and push people around."

"Yes Mr. Pitts."

"Are you hurt Mr. Pitts?"

"No thank goodness. If I were this young man would be in for a whopper of a lawsuit."

Peter was totally bewildered. He didn't know what was going on. All he could do was try to say he was sorry but he couldn't get the words out again.

"I'm...I'm... That is...I'm..."

"Look at him." said the man. "He's so mad he can't speak. All of you help me get my bags on the train and get away from this long haired weirdo. "

As the railroad workers gathered his bags and put him on all we could do was stand there and watch them. Pete stood there with shock.

As we comforted Peter and helped him gather his belongings I had to ask, "Anyone know who that was?"

"That was Garfield Pitts." said Bob. "He just inherited this railroad."

"He's the one who hired the group?"

"No that was the older man who is now boarding the train."

I looked towards the train to see a shorter man who was slightly bent over. He was bald on top and had white hair on the sides and back of his head. Except for being slightly bent over he looked in pretty good shape. He was talking to the conductor and they were having a good laugh.

"That nice old man is his Father?"

"Hard to believe isn't it?" said Bert. "But he started this railroad and it's been thriving till lately. Most travelers now prefer to travel by plane now."

"We better be going." Said Bob.

We said our goodbyes and then the five of us boarded the train.

Chapter 3

Once inside the train we split up and went our separate
ways. Micky and Davy were given a compartment to share
and Mike and Peter shared one next to them. I wondered if I
would have a compartment by myself or if I would have to
share one with a stranger. I didn't get the luxury of having a
compartment by myself. I didn't even get a compartment. I
was pushed like cattle into the press car. I got the lower berth
and the upper went to an overweight middle age reporter who
liked to eat in bed. Nothing wrong with that but with all he
had I felt like I could have lived a few days off the crumbs that
fell from his bunk on to mine that night. The next eight hours
was one of the roughest nights of my life. Between the rattling
of rails and being hit by the occasional crumb I hardly slept at
all. It must have been around 8am when I heard people getting
up. I pulled back the curtain that I had drawn the night before
and saw men getting dressed in the aisle way.

"This part wasn't covered in school." I thought to myself.

So I got out and did the same. Nothing seemed stranger
then a bunch of half naked men getting dressed together in an
aisle.

Soon I was making my way to the Dining Car for breakfast.
There I saw the guys seated at a table. Davy waved me over
and Micky pulled up another chair from the empty table next
to them. As I sat down we all said good morning. Mike was
giving me an odd look as I looked at the menu.

"Buddy you look like you slept in your clothes."

"It probably would have been better if I did." I said.

"Ah ha!" said Micky. "I guess they made you spend the night in the press car."

"Yeah, how did you know?"

"My Mom and Dad were entertainers. They told me stories of their traveling days."

It wasn't long before the car was filled with actors and business men. They were divided in half like a couple of cliques. The actors were on our side of the car and the business men were on the other side. One man was making the rounds of all the tables. Smiling and laughing and shaking hands. At the moment he was at the table of the networks #1 hit show The Ranchers. It was a family show set in the west about a mostly male family running a ranch. When I turned to look at him he was shaking hands with the star of the show Len White. He played the head of the family and had commute to the United States from Canada to do movies but moved here when he was cast in the TV show.

I turned back to see that the waiter had just brought us all glasses of water. I took a sip of water and then looked up and made eye contact with Mike.

"Who's that talking to Len White?"

"That's Brandon Parks. He's the President of programming for the network."

It was hard to tell since I was sitting down but Mr. Parks was well over six feet tall. He had jet black hair but it was starting to go gray. He looked like a man of his late 40's or early 50's who had kept in shape. He had a lean build and broad shoulders. Maybe it was just the suit that made him look that way but still I wouldn't want to have him angry with me.

He briefly stopped at the table of Samantha Strong who was eating with Jean Feldon the star of the sit-com I Remember Barbara. As he shook their hands and left them to their breakfast he headed toward us. As he arrived at our table he was all smiles and shook hands. He had a questioning look on his face as he shook my hand.

"So who do we have here? Is this an addition to the cast that I wasn't told about?"

"No it's Josh Adams. He's doing an article on us." Said Davy.

"Well Mr. Adams I'm sure you'll have a favorable article to write about them. With hit records and not only a hit show but an awarding winning one as best comedy series at the Emmys the network is quite proud of these four young men."

Micky looked up and again tried to sound like a Hollywood executive. "Yes B.P. I predict that these young men will go far, at least as far as the end of this railroad track."

Mike laughed then looked at Mr. Parks. "The TV show is nice but it's the music that's doing better than the show. You fought us on controlling our own music but we can sing Happy Birthday and it would sell millions."

Mr. Parks looked back toward him. "Now Mike you know that we had to be careful. We didn't know if this whole rock and roll/Beatle thing would be over before the show got on the air. At least now we know we are showing a comical mirror of today's youth to society."

With that Mr. Parks smiled at me and turned to leave.

"Way to go Mike," said Peter.

"Maybe I shouldn't have said anything. I just wanted to let him know he wasn't fooling anyone and Josh should know how the network felt at the beginning of the show."

Just then at the far end of the car barged Garfield Pitts. He looked as if he just wanted to walk straight through the car but was stopped by Brandon Parks. It was hard to hear that far away what was being said but it looked like Parks was insisting that he eat with him. Pitts looked disgusted but sat down at Parks table.

Just then the waiter returned to take our orders. Micky had beacon and eggs over easy. Davy ordered eggs over medium with biscuits. Mike asked for buttermilk pancakes with maple syrup and a side order of beacon. I ordered scrambled eggs and sausage links. Peter couldn't seem to find what he wanted on the menu. He looked at the waiter.

"Do you make your pancakes with wheat germ?"

"I don't think so sir."

"Do you have any granola?"

"No sir."

"I guess I'll just have a bowl of Kellogg's corn flakes with milk and a glass of orange juice."

"Very good sir."

With that the waiter left to tell the cook our order.

Just then a loud noise came from the end of the car. It sounded like someone pounding on a table. Everyone turned to see Parks pounding his fist on the table like a mad man. Pitts was waving his arms like crazy.

"No love's being lost at that table," said Davy.

Soon Pitts stood up and continued his walk through the car. His walk was at an even brisker pace then when he first entered. All eyes were on him till he got to the end and slammed the door close. Then everyone turned to finish their food and conversations at their tables.

For a moment all was silent at our table. I turned to look back at Mr. Parks. He was sitting there looking out the window. He absentmindedly wrung his hands and looked very nervous. Whatever that conversation was about upset him a great deal.

"Who had the buttermilk pancakes with maple syrup?" said a voice from behind me.

I turned to see the waiter had returned with our orders.

"I did." Said Mike.

Our orders were distributed to each of us. As we got our food we started to eat. Before eating I silently said grace. Then as I partook of my food I thought to myself that this train trip was starting to be more interesting than I thought it would.

Chapter 4

We finished our breakfast and tried to talk about the article but quickly realized that all of the people in the car were talking and making it hard to hear each other. Mike suggested that we move the meeting to his and Peter's compartment.

On the way out of the car I noticed a burly man sitting alone at a table. He had been sitting there the whole time and only had a cup of coffee sitting in front of him. He had a black mustache and was wearing a brown suit and hat with a yellow and brown striped necktie. As I passed him he moved slightly and his coat fell back a little bit to reveal a shoulder holster with a gun in it. I got little a closer and whispered to Mike.

"That man's got a gun."

"Yeah he looks like a railroad cop."

"Trains have their own cops?"

"Almost as long as the railroads have been around. "

As we went down the corridor we saw Garfield Pitts once again. He was with a much younger man who looked like he was about my age. The younger man had shoulder length sandy brown hair and was wearing a paisley shirt with blue jeans and sandals. Pitts was less animated then before but from the look on both their faces the conversation was heated. The corridor was small and both moved to the side as we all tried to pass by them. I was the last in line and heard the younger man call him Dad and said he didn't want something.

We got to Mike and Peter's compartment. I interviewed them as a group and took notes on what it was like to go from TV stars to music stars. It was really a fun interview session. These four didn't know each other when the series started but I could tell they had become best friends. Almost like brothers. We laughed a lot and even sang. They were just as entertaining in person as they were on the show.

Suddenly there was a knock at the door. Peter opened it and came face to face with Garfield Pitts.

"Oh it's you." Said Garfield, as he looked at Peter. "I hope you won't shove me again if I ask you to keep the noise down."

"Sorry if we're too noisy Mr. Pitts. We'll keep it down and I only wanted to shake your hand yesterday. I wasn't trying to shove you."

"You'll say anything to make yourself look good now won't you."

With that he took his leave of us. Peter closed the door. As he turned he looked at Mike.

"What is with that guy?"

"He's probably mad at something else and taking it out on you." Mike said.

We decided to cut out the singing. We continued the interview the rest of the morning. We would have kept going if it hadn't been for Micky.

"Anyone else starting to get hungry?"

They all agreed they were and started to go to the Dining Car. I wasn't too hungry yet so I decided to go to the back of the train and get some air. I was there for awhile when another gentleman joined me. He was a stocky man in a light brown suit. He was clean shaven and bald on top.

"Afternoon Joe!"

"You must have me mistaken for someone else. My name is Josh. Josh Adams"

"Pleased to meet you Josh, I'm Oliver Jackson."

We shook hands and both looked at the passing scenery for a little while. Then he decided to start a conversation.

"So what line of work are you in?"

"I'm a reporter. How about you?"

"Me? Oh I'm just a simple small business man. I'm into plastics."

"Really? I thought this train was just full of TV people."

"Well I am in television too. I have a small share in the network. TV is the wave of the future you know."

"So it would seem. I prefer to get my news through newspaper."

"Oh Joe the real wave is network news. Get out of the papers and into TV. You'll make a fortune."

"Maybe but I still like to have something to hold when I read the news."

We had a nice pleasant chat. The whole time when he had to use my name he kept calling me Joe. He was a nice man so I never bothered to correct him. Soon the conversation lulled and we were back to watching the scenery. I suppose he got bored and he decided to leave.

"Well I'll see you around the train Joe."

"I'll see you later Joe."

We both laughed but I don't think he cared for the joke. There was a quick flash of anger on his face as he turned and went back inside the train.

I stood out there for a few more minutes. Then I went back inside. As I did I saw Samantha Strong coming towards me. With her was an older gentleman who had thick white hair and even though he looked to be in his fifties he had kept in shape. He had the broad shoulders of a linebacker. Both were smiling as they approached. Samantha looked up and saw me.

"Hello! I saw you last night at the train station didn't I?"

"Yes, I'm Josh Adams."

"I'm…"

"Oh I know who you are Miss. Strong. I see your show every week."

"Well that's sweet. This is Henderson Pitts the second."

"Junior to my friends."

We shook hands.

"Any relation to…"

"Yes my Father use to own the railroad. My brother runs it now. Samantha I have to get back to my compartment. I'll see you later Mr. Adams."

"Oh if I can call you Junior you can call me Josh."

"Mr. Adams."

I watched him walk away. I heard Samantha sigh. I turned to look at her.

"You got him mad, which is a pretty easy thing to do these days."

"Why would he be mad?"

"He wanted the railroad but his younger brother got it."

"That would upset me too. Still I didn't know his situation."

"So what does Josh Adams do for a living?"

We walked a little further. I wondered what I should tell her. I was a little embarrassed to say that I wrote for a teen magazine.

"I'm a writer."

"What kind? Are you a scriptwriter?"

I had hoped she would let it go but she wants specifics.

"No I write for a new teen magazine. I doubt you have heard of it. The Fab Tab."

"Oh my of course I've heard of it. Before I left on this trip my Agent called and said they were to have someone interview me when I got back. Speaking of my Agent I need to see if there are any messages for me from him. I'll have to go to the radio operator."

She started to walk away. Then she turned back around. She tossed her beautiful long blonde hair. Her naturally bright red lips arched into a big smile that lit her big baby blue eyes.

"I do hope you'll be doing the interview Mr. Adams."

"Call me Josh."

"Well then I hope you'll be doing the interview Josh."

She turned again and walked away. As she did I could only think I hope so too.

Chapter 5

The rest of that day was fairly uneventful. With nothing to do but look at the passing scenery it was becoming very apparent why the traveling public now had decided to do most of their long distance traveling by plane. Night had fallen. I was not looking forward to having to spend another night in a box. Thankfully at the urging of Peter and Mike the porter got a cot and placed it in their compartment for me to sleep on. It made their compartment more cramped for them but it was a nice gesture from them and it was more room for me and no huge amounts of crumbs falling down on me in the darkness.

Still even with the extra room I didn't sleep well that night. One of the others didn't sleep well that night either. For the longest time I could hear them tossing and turning while trying to get into a comfortable position to sleep. Sleep eluded him however and I heard him get up and change into his clothes from his pajamas. He then quietly opened the door as not to disturb anyone as he left. I looked up to see which one it was. As the light from the hallway came in, through my blurry sleep deprived vision I could see it was Peter. He didn't see me and as he closed the door the room got darker and I tried to get back to sleep.

I don't know how long it had been between when I fell asleep and when the commotion in the hallway woke Mike and I up.

"What's all the noise about?" Asked Mike.

"I don't know."

We both got up. Mike opened the door and we both stood there in our pajamas looking at a lot of people running about. Micky and Davy were also standing in their door way in their sleep apparel as well. Davy caught the attention of a Porter.

"Excuse me sir! What's with all the romp and circumstance?"

He turned to him with wide eyes and just stared. He then looked towards Mike and me. I could see he was trying to think of the right words. Finally he looked back at Davy and just blurted it out.

"Someone's been killed."

He then turned and continued his run with the rest of the crowd. Almost in unison the four of us followed them.

The crowd started to slow down as we came to the Baggage car. Some of the crowd thinned out as they didn't want to take any chances by moving between the cars. As we got to the end the crowd surprisingly parted down the middle to make way for us. It was like Moses parting the Red Sea. I didn't understand why they wanted us to have a better view until I got to the front of the crowd. There, standing over the dead body was Peter. He was holding a gun and talking to the mustached railroad cop who was holding Peter at gunpoint. We slowly approached them with Mike in front.

"What's going on here Pete?"

"They think I killed him Mike."

"I don't think he killed him. I know he did," said the railroad cop.

"What is your name sir?"

He pulled his suit jacket back to show his badge.

"I'm Sgt. Frank Benton. I'm the cop on this railroad line. I came in here after I heard a shot and found him standing here with that gun in his hand."

"That's crazy. Peter isn't violent and even so who is there that he would have wanted dead?" Mike asked.

Just then we looked down at the body. He was lying on his stomach but his face was turned on his left side. Amidst the broken shards of glass and rags on the floor we saw the face of Garfield Pitts.

"Oh boy! It's Mr. Pitts."

Chapter 6

I could hear thunder from the storm that was approaching outside. It was nothing compared to the storm that was brewing inside the train. The flashes of light inside were coming from the cameras of the newspaper photographers that were on the train and not from the lightning from the storm. I'm not a photographer so I just took some mental notes for the article later.

Benton handcuffs Peter and takes him by the arm.

"Come on I'll have to lock you in my compartment with me for the rest of the trip."

Davy looks at Benton. "But Peter didn't do it. He's clean."

"That's true I shower every day."

Benton turns to look at Peter then turns his attention back to us.

"Look, Mike and I share a compartment with Peter. If you leave him with us we'll make sure that he is always watched. He'll always have at least one of us with him. He'll never be alone."

Benton looks at us with contempt. I can tell that he thinks he is smarter than us. I didn't think he would agree with my request but then he looked at me.

"Ok! But if he gets away I'll arrest you as accessories, in other words no monkey business."

Suddenly he realizes who is talking to.

"Pardon the expression fellas."

As we started to take Peter back to the compartment Micky looked at Peter's hands. He then looked at Benton.

"I think you can take the handcuffs off of him."

"He has to be handcuffed. He may try to overpower you and escape. I was told he even attacked Garfield Pitts at the train station."

The crowd starts to murmur. Above the murmurs I heard someone say that they saw it happen.

Just looking at Mike I can tell by his body language that he is getting really tired of this guy. Mike straightens his back up then walks directly up to him and with his finger pokes him in the shoulder.

"Now man listen. You obviously haven't seen our show or read anything about us. If you had you would know that Peter Tork is a fine upstanding citizen. He isn't the least bit violent and wouldn't even think of escape. The incident at the train station was just a misunderstanding. He'll prove his innocence legally. Besides even if he did take it on the run where could he go on a train?"

"You're right there is no other place to go. But you have to make sure that the door to the room is locked at all times."

With that Benton took off the handcuffs. As we walked the crowd parted way for us once more. The people looked at us with curiosity as we passed them. Some looked with anger as if they had already made up their minds about us. I say us because with me being about the same age as them and always hanging with them today they most likely thought I would side with the Monkees. They were correct. Only one face stood out from the crowd. That is the face of Samantha Strong. She stood there in a pink robe that was tied at the waist but during her walk must have loosened as I could see she was wearing short pink matching nightgown. Her thick long blond hair was tousled from having been sleeping until a few minutes ago. She gave me a smile that lit up her face. Once that smile was beaming my way I felt that all was right with the world. I just knew that we would find a way to clear Peter. I smiled back at her. The guys and I left the car and kept walking towards our compartment.

Chapter 7

Back in Mike and Peter's compartment Peter sat on the bottom bunk. I sat on my cot with Davy as we both faced Peter. Micky was leaning against the wall and looking out the window at the passing night scenery. Mike was pacing around the small area behind Davy and I.

"So what happened Pete?" asked Mike.

"Well I couldn't get to sleep so I changed my clothes and left our room to go to the Baggage Car."

"I can vouch for him on that. I looked up to see him leave the room." I said.

"Why did you go to the Baggage Car?" asked Davy.

"Because when I can't sleep I play my guitar till I get tired. My acoustic was packed away and in the Baggage Car. I went to get it and was just going to play it there till I got sleepy."

"Well Mr. Pitts is taking a permanent nap now," said Micky.

Mike stopped pacing. "So what happened once you got there?"

Peter held his head in his hands and was quiet while he thought. Then he looked up. He looked past me and at Mike who was standing behind me.

"Well I went inside the car and it was dark. I didn't know where the light switch was so I left the door open so I could have some light. I didn't have it for long as that was when I heard the door slam shut. I continued trying to feel my way along but I didn't get far. I tripped over something. Well now I know it was Mr. Pitts body but I didn't know it at the time. With my hand I felt something next to where I fell and as I got up I was still holding it. That's when Benton came in. He saw the body and me holding a gun and arrested me."

Still leaning against the wall Micky turned his attention from the scenery and towards Peter.

"Hey that's great Pete!"

All of us are stunned as we slowly turn towards Micky. It's Mike who voices our thoughts.

"How is that great? He's caught holding a gun that may be the weapon that killed Mr. Pitts."

"Yeah but it's all circumstantial."

"Hey you're right. There was no witness."

"Yeah even Benton isn't really a witness."

"Yeah he just…" Mike suddenly got a sad look on his face. Then all five of us joined together in the thought. "… saw Peter holding the gun."

"Yeah well others may think Peter did it but he's our friend. We know he didn't. Peter just told us the truth." Said Micky.

"But we have to find a way to clear his name."

"We don't have to clear his name. It's clean. We have to find the one with the …well the one with … you know the one with the dirty name."

"You mean the real killer."

"Are you crazy?"

Davy joins in the conversation. "Yeah we're entertainers not detectives."

With a sad look that tugs at your heart Peter looks at us.

"Guys, I'm scared. I didn't kill him. I'd never hurt anyone."

With looks that show they feel ashamed of themselves the other Monkees put their hands on his shoulder. Micky looks Peter directly in the eye.

"Don't worry Pete. We'll find out who did this."

"Yeah if we have anything to say about this you won't do one day in a real jail," says Davy.

I looked at him and said, "I'll do what I can to help them too."

A smile comes to Peter's face. He now seems to have more confidence in his fate.

"Thanks guys. With you guys helping I know we'll find the real killer."

"What do you mean helping ?" I asked.

"Well I'm going to be looking into it too."

"Now Peter," said Davy, "he's right you know. You can't look into this because you can't leave this room."

"Well I don't want to just sit around here and wait."

"If you're seen leaving this room you'll just make matters worse."

Resigning himself to his current situation Peter decides to lie down on his bunk.

Mike looks at all of us. "Now we have to decide how to go about this."

We went round and round about what to do but we kept coming to the same conclusion. That was that there wasn't much to look into since the only witness was Peter. Dawn was now coming and as the rays of the sun started to shine through the clouds we could tell we were near Gallup, New Mexico. We were all very depressed. Peter more than anyone.

Suffering from lack of sleep and realizing that I had to get on with the day I went to the dining car for some coffee. Just as I was about to take my seat near the door I saw Samantha Strong. She was sitting farther down the car with her back to me. As I approached her I could see she was wearing white pumps to match her white miniskirt. Her top was royal blue and was outlined in white. Her long blond hair flowed down over her shoulders. Just as I got to the table I could see she was drinking a cup of black coffee. Then she looked up at me. She seemed surprised to see me.

"Oh! Hello Josh. I didn't expect to see anyone else here so early."

"I haven't slept all night. I thought I would get some coffee. Mind if I join you?"

"Not at all, have a seat."

As I sat down she looked at me with her big blue eyes.

"So why are you up so early?" I asked.

"Just a habit I got into with needing to be at the studio for early make up calls. I think I know why you couldn't sleep."

"Well I think everyone knows that. We had Peter telling us everything that happened. Even though I believe he's innocent there doesn't seem to be any other witness to know that Peter didn't kill him."

"I'm sure that there are plenty of people who wish they had done it."

"How do you know?"

"Garfield Pitts always advertised himself as a business man and a family man but when he saw some pretty girl that all went out the window."

"Did he hit on you?"

"Big time. His family owns stock in the network my show is on. He always stopped by to watch us film my show. When we were finished he always asked me for a date. I kept telling him I wasn't interested in him and even if I was I still wouldn't go with him since he was married."

"Didn't that make him stop?"

"No he just said that he liked a challenge and tried even harder. Then he started trying blackmail."

"What did he have against you?"

"Nothing bad. It was just that I was up for a co-starring role in the Matt Helm movie that came out last year."

"I saw that movie. I didn't see you in it."

"Exactly! I was supposed to sign the contract and the day before Garfield asked me out again and again I turned him down. He said he knew I was about to sign the contract for the role and he knew someone at the studio. He would make sure that I didn't get the part if I didn't go with him that night. I thought he was bluffing and still said no. The next day, just as I was getting ready to meet with my agent, I got a call. It was my agent and he said the studio decided they didn't want me in this movie or any movie that was about to go into production. It could have been my big break in films and he made sure it was taken away from me."

"How do you know it just wasn't a coincidence?"

"I saw him later in the day and he was gloating about it. He asked me out again saying he could make the studio change their minds. I still said no. I want to be a movie star but my reputation means more to me."

I had to smile. It was nice to see someone in Hollywood who put their morals before their career. Still she did give me something to think about.

Just then Davy walked up to our table.

"Hello mates!"

"Davy!"

"Hello David! Have a seat."

Davy slid in and sat next to Samantha.

"Did Josh tell you that we are looking into the murder case?"

"He said you were talking about it all night but Peter didn't see any other witnesses."

"That's true but when a mates in trouble you don't give up so easy."

Samantha smiled.

"Well Davy it's nice to know you're so loyal to your friends."

"Well if you aren't they won't be your friends for long."

Seeing that Davy was looking more favorable to her I had to interject.

"I was going to keep digging into it too."

"I know you will Josh. Now if you two will excuse me I need to go."

"Is it something we said love?"

"I don't think either of you could say anything that would want to make me leave. I just have to read a script for Espionage so I'm ready to shoot it when I'm back in Hollywood."

With that she turned and left and we watched her walk to the end of the car.

"Too bad she had to go. I really like her."

"I know you do." I said.

"I'm just a red blooded single male. Besides you have a crush on her too."

"Well she is attractive. I hate to say it but she gave me reason to believe that she may know more about this killing."

"How so?"

I told Davy what she had told me.

Chapter 8

A few minutes later Davy and I had taken our cups of coffee back to the compartment along with cups for Mike, Micky and Peter. We also had a fresh pot for refills. As we calmly drank our coffee I filled in the others what I told Davy. Mike was the first to speak.

"So she has a motive."

"Yeah she does but I hate to think of her as the killer."

"Well we do too," said Micky. "After all we know her a little better then you and we consider her a friend."

"Yeah," said Peter. "I sometimes have lunch with her at the commissary."

"Guys we will have to keep our eyes and ears open," Mike said. "There may be others on this train who wished Mr. Pitts ill."

Peter turned toward him with a puzzling look.

"Ill? He wasn't sick."

"Not ill like he was sick Pete. I meant like...bad. You know like...well dead."

"Oh! Well they got that."

After we finished our drinks and talk Mike, Micky and I decided to circulate amongst the passengers of the train. I first contacted a Porter who directed me where I could go to send a message to my editor. In the message I told him of Peter's situation. I also told him that in order to clear him of any wrongdoing he shouldn't print anything till I had the whole story. Otherwise someone who knows the real killer may send them a message back and inform them of our progress. Being new to the paper I hoped that my editor could be trusted to not rush it into print. I also asked him if he could find out info on the others on the passenger list with their relationship with Garfield Pitts.

Walking down the hall I had to excuse myself between Micky and Len White and Jean Feldon. Micky told me exactly how the conversation went.

After leaving Mike and Peter's compartment Micky saw Len leaving his compartment and meeting with Jean Feldon who was waiting outside his door. Micky's parents are showbiz veterans and knew Len through them. He had been a movie star in the 40's and early 50's and Micky's Dad had been in a couple of movies with him. He didn't know Jean as well but had seen her around the studio. He also wasn't too surprised to see them together as he had read in the papers they were having an affair.

"Hi Len, Jean!"

"Hello Mick," said Len. "How's Peter holding up?"

"He's upset but doing well considering the situation. What situation he is considering is anyone's guess since he's so quiet. Perhaps it's the trouble in the middle east?"

"Peter is such a dear, sweet person," said Jean. "I don't see how he could kill anyone."

"He didn't. He just went in to get his guitar and tripped over the body."

"Well I know it's not nice to speak ill of the dead but getting shot couldn't happen to a better person." Said Len.

Micky looked at Len and asked him what he meant.

"Well Garfield Pitts was always hitting on Jean here."

"Yes, he was just awful."

"One day I saw him manhandling her and I pulled him away from her and punched him in the mouth. He didn't take too kindly to that and assumed that she and I were having an affair. I guess that made up story was his way of trying to ease his bruised ego. I've known Jean and her parents since she was a little girl. She's like a daughter to me. She told me about him. I told her to just ignore him but I saw that didn't work."

"Mr. Pitts said he would tell the papers about us having an affair."

"He bragged about how it would ruin my marriage. I told him my wife wouldn't believe it because she trusted me and she was friends with Jean as well."

"Then he said that the news would ruin both of our television careers."

"I didn't really care about myself. My show is always in the top 5 and probably would continue and I was considering retiring when the show ended anyway. But Jean's career is just starting. This was the first year of her sit-com. She could be a huge star and I didn't want that ruined. So I asked what he wanted."

"What did he want?"

"A date with Jean. I told him that was out of the question. So he left and the next day it hit the papers. My show dipped a bit but rebounded a few weeks later and I already told my wife what to expect."

"But my show nearly hit rock bottom, "said Jean. "The network almost canceled the show at mid-season."

"I told them I would leave my show if hers was canceled. So they let it run the rest of the season," said Len. "They were still deciding what the fall schedule would be like the day this train was leaving."

"The show's rating improved but not enough for it to be guaranteed that it would be renewed for next season. I guess I'll find out when I get back."

It was there that the conversation pretty much came to an end. As Len and Jean left Micky saw Jean starting to tear up. Len put a comforting arm around her shoulders. All Micky could do was wonder if the story was true.

Chapter 9

Meanwhile, Mike said he had a hard time getting to talk to anyone. He walked the length of the train trying to start conversations. But no matter how many times he smiled and tipped his hat to the ladies or shook hands with the men they all just smiled and turned away. Then, standing between the cars, he saw Henderson Pitts Sr.

"Mr. Pitts sir," said Mike quietly so not to startle the older gentleman.

Turning and looking as if he was just waking up from a dream the older gentleman looks up at the taller young man.

"Oh! Yes Mr.....eh..."

"Nesmith. Mike Nesmith. Are you sure you should be standing here between these cars? This train is moving awfully fast."

"Well Mr. Nesmith I've been standing between the cars watching the scenery go by long before you were even thought of. I always brought my sons on my trips. I would stand between the cars and watch the scenery with them. The look of joy and wonder they had in their eyes to see this country as it raced by them. The wind as it blew through their hair. They both loved it. Garfield seemed to love it even more. I remember the first time I saw him move his head with the rhythm of the wheels as they ran down the tracks. It was then I knew he was the one who loved the railroad as much as I do.

"It sounds like you enjoyed traveling with your sons."

"I did very much. I came out here today to remember the good times but I just feel sad."

"Well that's only natural sir considering what happened. I'm really sorry that it happened but Peter didn't have anything to do with it."

"Oh you must be one of those Mercies."

"Monkees. We're a band and have sit-com on the network that you own stock in. But that doesn't have anything to do with this. It's just that the guys all feel terrible about what happened but we need to find who really killed your son. Is there anyone who would want your son dead?"

"Not long ago I would have laughed at such a thought young man. In recent weeks however things have changed. You see Garfield loved the business He was always helping me and my oldest son to manage it. Jr. was a bit cold and aloof with the workers but Garfield got along well with them. If there was a problem with management and labor Garfield was always able to get them together. We are the only railroad line that has never had a strike and that is in part due to Garfield. Everyone loved him. But recently all that has changed. He'd gotten erratic. He was easily angered. He made bad business decisions and recently has been talking about dumping the TV network stock. If you're looking for someone who had a reason to kill him you may have a train full. Now if you'll excuse me Mr. Nesmith. My health is failing me. That's the reason I gave the company to Garfield so soon. I have a heart problem and I have to go to my car to get my medicine."

Chapter 10

After I saw Micky with Len and Jean I passed Junior Pitts. I tried to make conversation with him but he snubbed me. Considering how I accidentally angered him in our first meeting and now my new friend Peter is thought to have killed his brother I didn't blame him. I saw Oliver Jackson in his compartment as he had his door open. I thought of knocking on his door to see if he would talk. However, he was deep into reading some papers so I didn't interrupt. I decided to look into the baggage car. Maybe if I examined the scene of the crime I may get a clue to what happened.

As I opened the door in the more light of day I noticed things I couldn't see the night of the murder. There were rows and rows of luggage and suitcases. In the middle of one of the rows was an outline of how Garfield Pitts was found lying that night. Shattered glass that looked to be from some sort of bottle and rag was lying nearby. I knelt down to get a closer look at the glass. Suddenly I heard a noise. I started to get up and was half of the way turned around to see where it came from when I felt some pain above my temple. Just then the lights went out.

I woke up after feeling a splash of water on my face. Mike, Micky, Davy and Benton were looking over me. Micky and Davy helped me to my feet. As I rubbed the side of my head I could feel a lump already starting to grow.

"What happened?" I asked sounding like number one son from an old Charlie Chan movie.

"That's what we want to ask you," said Davy.

"Yeah," said Micky. "we've been looking for you for hours."

"Hours! How long have I been out?"

"Well the last time we saw you it was morning," said Mike.

"It's now evening. What time did you come in here and what were you doing in here?" said Benton.

I started to answer but I was suddenly surprised by Benton being there.

"Why are you here? Don't tell me you were concerned for me."

"The door was locked to the car and they wanted to see if you were in here. Now what were you doing in here?"

"I came in because I was hoping to find a clue to the real killer.

"The real killer is already in custody in your compartment. Don't make me sorry for letting him stay there."

"Hey who is with Peter?"

"That would be Samantha," said Mike. "She volunteered to be with him when she saw how concerned we were about finding you."

"That was nice of her. Hey, who threw water on me?"

"That would be me," said Benton.

I looked at his left hand and saw him holding a Styrofoam cup.

"And it wasn't water. It was Pepsi cola. You owe me a soft drink."

"Anyway I saw the outline and I knelt down to get a closer look at a piece of glass."

"What glass?"

"The glass around the outline."

I looked down and only saw the outline. The glass was all gone.

"It was here. There were shards of glass around the top of the outline."

The Monkees looked at me and all smiled.

"Why are you smiling?"

"Congratulations!" said Mike.

Micky looked at me with a bit of a frown and in his best over educated British accent said, "It's elementary my dear Joshua. You found a clue to the real killer."

Chapter 11

The guys helped me back to the compartment. When I got there I saw Samantha sitting on my cot. Across from her was Peter sitting on the bottom bunk. Samantha looked mad when she saw me coming in the room but turned sympathetic when she heard that I had been hit on the head.

"How did it happen?"

"I was hit when I was looking closer at some glass around the body's outline when I was in the baggage car."

"Dig this," said Davy. "When he woke up the glass was missing."

"What's that mean?"

"That means it was important enough for the real killer to knock out Josh and take it from him," said Mike.

Samantha started to look closer at the bump on my head.

"There's a small scratch on this bump. It could become infected. Do you have any peroxide and bandages?"

"No we didn't bring anything like that with us."

"Well I did. My Mother always told me to be prepared. I'll go to my room and be right back."

She kissed my bump and left the room.

Peter looked at me. "She is so sweet. How can you guys suspect her of murder?"

"She does have a motive."

Mike then looked at us and said, "What we need to concentrate on guys is to find the answer to the question why that glass was important to the killer?"

"Maybe he hit him over the head with a bottle before he shot him," said Davy.

"Maybe but why hit him first? He's got a gun so why not just shoot him?"

Peter is starting to pace around the room. He stops once to look out the window then starts to pace again.

"Guys this room is starting to close in on me. Isn't there any way I can get out of here for a few minutes?"

Davy stands up and looks at Peter.

"Well you're supposed to be under house arrest but he did say one of us had to be with you at all times. I suppose we can get out if I'm with you."

Peter looks at Mike, Micky and I. He has a gleam in his eyes that he hasn't had since the murder.

"We'll be back later guys."

With that Peter grabs Davy by the arm and practically drags him out of the room. I lie down trying to nurse my head while Micky sits there and listens to Mike wonder why Garfield Pitts was hit with a bottle first then shot.

Chapter 12

Davy and Peter are walking to the end of the train. Peter is getting mean looks from some of the people that he passes. Some actually smile at him. After one woman smiles Peter looks at Davy.

"You would almost think that some of these people were glad he was dead."

"From what I have heard a lot of them are."

"You would think that there would be at least one person who would be mourning him."

Just then they came to the end of the train. They could see on the outside deck a stocky man in a white business suit with a hat. He is with a younger man dressed in bellbottoms and a bright colored floral shirt. The older man was patting the younger man on the shoulder. As they opened the door they heard the last part of their conversation.

"…he was a good business man and I'm sure that he loved you."

"Sometimes I think that he loved his business more."

The older man turns around to see Davy and Peter.

"Well hello Joe."

"My name isn't Joe. I'm David and this is Peter."

"I know this is just how I greet everyone. It saves me some embarrassment if I forgot their name. I'm Oliver Jackson and this young man here is young Mr. Pitts. I was just comforting him in the loss of his Father."

Peter looks at the young man.

"I'm so sorry about your Dad."

"It's ok. Don't worry I don't believe that you're the one who killed him."

Oliver looks at the young man. "Well this deck is getting crowded. I think you'll be safe with David here."

As he left, Peter looked at Davy.

"He must think I'm guilty because it's only safe if you're here."

The younger man stares out into space not even seeing the countryside that he is passing.

"He wasn't a good man. He wasn't that good of a Father either. So why is it now I can only remember the times we tossed a baseball and he took me to the movies?"

Davy looks over at him. "Well we always seem to remember the good times instead of the bad when a loved one dies…eh…"

"Jake my name is Jake. Look I know my Dad wasn't a saint and he never understood me. I wasn't interested in business. I wanted to be a teacher or social worker but he insisted that I join the family business."

"You don't like running a railroad?"

"No railroad is old generation. The only part of the business I liked was the television network. My family owns most of the stock. Television can be a great teaching tool. Look I'm not feeling well. If you'll excuse me I want to lie down."

"Sure," said Peter.

"If you ever need to talk just look us up," said Davy.

As Jake left Peter watched as he walked away.

"Boy! I feel sorry for him."

"I don't know if we should be," Davy said as he looked at the passing countryside.

"Why not?"

"With his Father dead he probably inherits all or part of the business."

"But he said he hated running the railroad."

"But he did say he liked owning most of the stock in the TV network. He has a motive."

Chapter 13

I had just left my compartment where Davy and Peter filled us all in on their meeting with Jake. I was just walking past Samantha's door when we nearly bumped into each other as she came out.

"Oh sorry about that," she said.

"I'm back up on my feet and you nearly swept me off them again."

She giggled an embarrassed laugh as she joined me in my walk.

"So how is your head?"

"It still hurts but I think I'll live."

"So where are you going?"

"Not too many places to go on a train. I've been lying down nursing my head for awhile. I just thought I would stretch my legs."

From behind I hear someone following us. Suddenly his pace increases. He is coming at us faster. I am just about to turn around to see who it is when I hear a voice.

"Mr. Adams! Mr. Adams!"

I turn to see one of the Porters walking towards me at a brisk pace.

"Yes, I'm Josh Adams."

"I have a message for you."

He hands the message to me. As I open it and start to read it the Porter leaves. I can't believe what it says. I hope that Samantha can't see it and I try to not show the expression on my face but I must not have done a good job.

"What is it? Why so worried?"

"Probably nothing. My editor just wants to see the progress I'm making on my article. It's my first job so I better go back and get what I have and wire it back to him. Don't want to find out I'm out of work when I get back."

We said our goodbyes and I hurried back to my room. Not to get the article, which I had barely started, but to show the guys what the message really said.

When I got to the room only Mike and Peter were there. They said that Micky and Davy had gone to their compartment next door. I quickly went and got them. Once we were all together I read them the message. It really was from my editor but it wasn't about my article.

"I asked him to find anything that he could about the other passengers on this train," I told them.

"What did he find out?" asked Mike.

"There is only information about one passenger. It says that the police suspect that the killer of Paul White may be on this train."

"Who's Paul White?" asked Micky.

"Isn't he that guy who was in the news the day the train left?" asked Davy.

"Yeah what was that for?" inquired Micky.

"I remember," said Mike. "He made the papers because he was murdered."

"Great!" said Peter. "Now there are two killers on the train."

"Well no matter what, guys we need to really be alert now."

"I don't know. What are the odds that there would be two killers on the train?" Asked Mike.

"I know what you mean Mike but we still have to consider the possibility."

When I came in earlier Peter was looking kind of sullen. But suddenly the dark cloud seemed to have lifted and he looked a little brighter.

"Have you told Benton yet? This could get suspicion off of me."

"Not yet I wanted to tell you guys."

"Well let's tell him now."

"I'm sure the police probably already contacted him."

"Well then let's go ask him."

Seeing that hopeful look on his face we all caved in.

"Ok! Anyone know where he is?"

"I'll ask a Porter."

Peter looked out the door but didn't see anyone. So we decided to all go together and find one. Halfway through the train we found a Porter who said the last he saw Benton was in the front car. We continued on our way. The tracks were getting a little rougher and with all the shaking it was hard to keep our balance. Finally, we got to the second car from the front and there was Benton walking toward us. Before we got any closer or said anything I could see the scowl on his face. He raised his hand and pointed a finger at us.

"WHAT IS HE DOING OUT OF HIS COMPARTMENT???" He yelled.

"Relax," I said. "We're all still with him."

"His compartment is supposed to be his jail while he is on this train. You don't see the guards at the state penitentiary taking prisoners out for a stroll around the block."

"Well having him stay in his compartment may be a thing of the past. Read this."

I handed him the message. I tried to read the expression on his face but it never changed. He had the same scowl that he did when we entered the car. Then he looked up and handed it back.

"Well?"

"Well what? This changes nothing. For all I know he may have killed White."

"That's not possible," said Davy.

"Why not?"

"Because I remember reading the article and it said he was found dead at 9am and was dead at least an hour and Peter met with me for breakfast at 8 o'clock in the morning that day."

"I'm supposed to take the word of a man who promised to keep the prisoner in his compartment but now is taking him for a walk. Get him back in his compartment and keep him there."

With that Benton shoved the paper back into my hand and stormed off.

"Sorry Pete."

"That's ok Davy. Let's go back."

Chapter 14

Mike and Peter went back to their compartment. Davy and Micky went back to theirs and invited me in.

"What is wrong with Benton?" I asked.

"When some people think that they have the answer they won't let go," said Micky.

"They see you have long hair and play rock and roll music so you must be the bad guy," said Davy as he flopped himself down on the lower berth.

"Well once the real cops get involved they'll see Peter has an alibi for the White murder."

"I hope so."

"What do you mean you hope so Davy? You said you had breakfast with Peter at the time of the murder."

"I did but the reason I remember the article is that it was around the corner from where we had breakfast and Peter was a little bit late. It was almost 8:30 when he arrived."

"Great! What else can go wrong?"

"I don't think Peter even knows this White guy. So he really doesn't have a motive and you have to have a motive to murder someone," said Micky.

"That's true but just bumping into someone isn't much of a motive to kill either. Yet they seem to want to use that to frame Peter for Pitts murder," said Davy.

"Well he was holding the gun," I said.

Micky and Davy quickly turned to me. If looks could kill I would be the latest person dead on this train.

"Come on now, you know I don't think he did it. I'm just saying that it looks bad to be holding the murder weapon."

"We know," said Micky. "It's just this is a pretty stressful situation when your friend is accused of murder."

"I know. I think I'll go next door so you two can get some rest."

As I went to my compartment I wondered where Peter could have been that day for nearly a half-an-hour. I thought maybe I could talk to him. As I entered I saw Mike and Peter talking. Mike looked up.

"Hey shotgun! Glad to see you. I thought I'd get something to drink."

"But he couldn't because he had to babysit me," said Peter.

"Why didn't you just ask a Porter to get you one?"

"I just want to get one myself. You guys want anything?"

"Coke for me," said Peter.

"I'll have a Sprite."

"Ok, I'll be back soon."

I plopped down in the chair next to Peter. Peter picked up a magazine to read and propped up his feet.

"Man!" He said. "That war in Vietnam looks like it will never end."

"I know. We need to keep the communist at bay so they don't come here but that war seems like a losing cause. We should bring our guys back home. But to discuss matters closer to home…"

"I'd rather not."

"I understand Pete but I have to know. Why were you almost a half-an-hour late meeting Davy for breakfast that morning?"

"I knew he would tell you. I overslept."

"Well that could happen to anyone. Was there anyone who saw you leaving late?"

"Not that I can remember."

"Did you ever meet that Mr. White?"

"I don't think so."

"Then you're probably in the clear on this murder. You didn't know him so you would have no reason to kill him."

"Too bad you didn't see anyone who would know that you overslept."

Chapter 15

While Peter and I were talking in the compartment, Mike was sitting at a table in the dining car waiting for the Coke that he ordered. The waiter approached his table with the drink. When he got there he put a glass of ice on the table and took the open bottle of Coca-cola and poured it into the glass.

"Hey thanks man. That will hit the spot," said Mike.

The waiter placed the half empty bottle on his tray and started to take it back.

"Wait a minute buddy. I'm paying for the whole bottle so just leave the bottle."

The waiter placed the bottle on the table as Mike looked up at him.

"Can you also bring me another bottle of Coke and one of Sprite to take back to my roommates?"

"I suppose so sir."

With that the waiter turns to leave.

Before Mike could take his first sip Henderson Pitts the second takes the seat facing Mike. Mike looks up with surprise at the uninvited guest at his table.

"You don't mind if I join you do you Mr. Nesmith?"

"No Mister…"

"Pitts, Henderson Pitts the second."

"Oh that's right. You're…"

"The brother of the man your friend is supposed to have killed."

"I'm glad you said suppose to have killed."

"I believe in innocent until proven guilty, besides there are plenty of men and women who would have wanted my brother dead."

"I know," said Mike as he took a drink. He set the glass down and gave Pitts a curious look.

"I know that look and I understand. I know you and your friends have been asking questions. You probably have me at the top of your list of suspects but I didn't kill my brother. We didn't get along and had different ways of doing business but I loved him and only wanted the best for him."

"But you're the oldest son. You were next in line to inherit the business. Yet when your Father retired he passed over you to your kid brother and gave him the family business."

"Dad thought my brother loved the business more. At the time it made sense. As much as I wanted the business I understand my Father's actions. I probably would have done the same thing if I was in his position."

"Still that must have stung. Most family businesses go to the oldest son."

"Look I just sat down for a friendly talk. Not to be accused of murder."

"Ok, I'm sorry. What did you want to talk about?"

"I know that your two friends talked to my nephew. If you're thinking that he did it you can forget it. That boy may dress weird but…"

"I don't think he dresses weird."

"No I guess you wouldn't. Anyway he is not a killer. He's peaceful and only wants to make the world a better place. His Father was that way once but something changed him. I don't know what but I do know his son isn't a killer."

"I hope he isn't but only time will tell."

Henderson Pitts the second gets up to leave. He starts to walk away but after a couple of steps he turns around and looks at Mike.

"I don't think I like you Mr. Nesmith. I hope you find who killed my brother but if you accuse me or anyone in my family I will come down on you like a hammer does a nail. None of us did it."

With that he turned and walked away. Mike drank his soft drink in peace.

Chapter 16

Not long after that Mike was back in the compartment with our soft drinks. My Sprite was slightly warmer then I liked it but still drinkable. He told us of his conversation in the dining car with Pitts Jr.

"Sounds like he sure was adamant," I said.

"Makes you wonder doesn't it?" said Peter.

"Wonder what?" asked Mike.

"I guess what adamant means," answered Peter.

I just smiled as I looked at Peter.

"I meant it sounds like he is unshakable in his position that his family didn't do it. But it does sound like he's hiding something. Maybe one of them did do it."

"That's what I thought but he may just have been defending his family," said Mike.

"Yeah if my brother was in that position I would stand up for him," said Peter.

"It still sounds odd to me. We already know that Junior and his nephew had motives. Did they have opportunity?"

"It was in the middle of the night," said Peter. "Almost everyone had opportunity."

"What about the Father? I wonder if he had a reason."

With that Mike looked up at me.

"That sweet old man? I don't think he would harm a fly."

"Maybe, but you need to have a bit of a killer instinct to get ahead in business. From what I saw at the station he seems to care about his employees. If his son led him to think he cared for them and then showed that he didn't care for them after he got control of the company then it could have led him to murder."

Mike just shook his head and looked down at the floor. He mumbled something under his breath that sounded like "hassle take off."

"What do you mean hassle take off!! Are you mad at me?"

"No I'm not mad. I said hostile takeover. He could have done a hostile takeover and gotten his company back. He wouldn't have to kill his own son."

"You can't do a hostile takeover if the person won't sell their stock in the company."

Just then the train shook. It was so violent that it tossed the three of us about the room.

"What was that?"

"I don't know let's see."

We opened the door and looked out into the aisle. Heads were popping out from every doorway.

Micky was looking out his door and turned to Mike.

"What was that?"

"I don't know," said Mike. "We were just wondering the same thing."

"Here comes the Porter. Maybe he knows. Excuse me Sir!"

"Yes Mr. Dolenz."

"Why have we stopped?"

"There seems to be a problem with the engine. That's all I know."

"Well I'm going to get out and stretch my legs and get some fresh air."

"I wouldn't do that Mr. Dolenz unless you're an expert high diver."

"What do you mean?"

"Look out your window."

We all rushed to our windows. As we looked out we saw the train was stalled on a bridge. What looked to be thousands of feet below was a river and some very rocky terrain.

"Wow! We really are stuck here."

"Can we move or will that shake the train too much?" asked Peter.

"Yes the train is in good shape and the bridge is very sturdy."

With that the Porter excused himself and continued on his way.

"Well guys I think I'll see how Micky and Davy are doing."

As I entered the aisle I saw that Micky left their door open so I just walked in. Micky was still looking out their window and Davy was picking up pieces of a broken bottle. I could see the label. It was black and I could make out the word Yardley on what was left.

"What happened?"

Davy looked up.

"Oh Hi! A bottle of aftershave fell over when the train stopped."

"You know seeing those broken pieces of glass remind me of that clue I found in the baggage car. Why was there a broken bottle next to the body?"

"Maybe Pitts dropped it when he fell," said Micky without turning his attention from the window.

"That wouldn't explain why someone knocked me out and stole the broken remains."

"Pitts may have broken it by using it as a weapon on his killer," said Davy.

"Still, why would the person steal the remains?"

Micky finally turned away from the window.

"Maybe he cut the guy and it had the killer's blood on it and he didn't want it tested for his blood type."

"If that's the reason maybe the killer has a rare blood type. That could definitely tell us who the killer is."

"We have to find that glass," said Davy.

"He may have thrown it away by now."

"We still have to keep an eye out for it just in case," said Micky.

Chapter 17

With the train not moving, the tension level inside rose to almost unbearable levels. Before, everyone seemed ok. Sure there was a killer on board and I suspect that most of them knew Peter couldn't have been the one. Still they were comforted that someone was in custody and the train would arrive in Clarksville soon. There some resolution would be found. But now the train was stalled high on top of a bridge. Night was coming and the real killer was still on the loose. It was starting to feel like anything could happen.

We were all getting hungry so Micky, Davy and I went to dinner and promised to bring something back for Peter and Mike. We made our way to the dining car as an uneasy silence seemed to encompass the train. We sat and ordered our meal. I kept wondering about this whole trip. Here I was covering these four men who were only actors and musicians on a trip to perform for one of their bosses. Then one of them is accused of murder. The one thing that kept tugging at my mind was those missing pieces of glass. Was it because the killer's blood was on it? If not, then why take them?

Our food came and we quickly ate our meals. The Dining car was full but the only sound was that of the cutlery hitting the plates. Soon we were finished and once the waiter brought 2 more meals for Mike and Peter we all got up in unison to leave.

On the way out I bumped into Oliver Jackson coming in. As I did I felt his hand touch the inside of my pocket. I thought it was an accident but before I could say anything to him about it Oliver said something.

"Sorry about that," he said.

Suddenly he seemed to notice Micky and Davy were with me.

"Well if it isn't the Joes! I hear you're trying to prove your friend is innocent. How's that coming along?"

"We've been asking some questions and have a few clues," said Davy.

"But until we come to a conclusion we think it should be kept between the five of us," said Micky.

"Of course I understand," answered Oliver.

"Say Mr. Jackson, I don't think we've talked to you about what you were doing at the time of the murder," I said.

"Me? Why would you think I had anything to do with the killing?"

"Everyone's a suspect till we find the real killer," said Micky.

"Well I'm afraid I don't have much of an alibi. I'm traveling alone and since it happened late at night I was asleep. I'm sure that's what most of the people on board were doing till the news spread to their car."

"Did you know the deceased in any way?" I asked.

"Only casually, I have stock in the network and his family does too. I saw him at some stockholder meetings when his Dad couldn't make it. Any other questions? If not I am very hungry and would like to get dinner before they stop serving."

We couldn't think of any at the moment and we continued back to our compartments and Oliver went to eat dinner. I was behind Micky and Davy as we walked in single file. As I have a habit of doing sometimes, I put my hands in my pockets. Usually they are empty except for my keys or wallet. This time I felt something in one that I didn't expect to feel. I pulled out a note. I unfolded it to see what it said.

"Joe,

Meet me at 3am on the back observation platform. I have some information you may be interested in.

Oliver Jackson"

It looked like I would have a more in-depth conversation with Mr. Jackson after all. I decided to keep quiet about the note till I heard him out. No need to alert the others. After all it may just be a business deal he wanted to talk about.

We got back to the compartment and gave Mike and Peter their meals. Later we all told jokes and sang some songs to pass the time. The others got tired and Micky and Davy went back to their compartment to sleep. Mike and Peter went to sleep also, but I just lay awake on my cot waiting for 3am. I didn't even bother to change my clothes.

From the moonlight shining through the window I could see on my watch that it was 2:50am. I quietly got up to go meet Oliver Jackson. Suddenly there was a loud scream. It woke Mike and Peter up and they both jumped out of bed. The three of us were quickly in the aisle way outside our door where Micky and Davy were already at and looking in the direction of the scream. Other heads began popping out the doors along the aisle. The five of us followed it till we came to see it was coming from Jean Feldon. Micky went over and put his arm around her shoulders.

"Jean what's wrong?"

Jean put her right hand over her mouth and calmed down. She was still so excited she wasn't able to speak. She just held her left arm straight out and pointed to the open door of one of the trains' compartments. Micky turned his attention in that direction. His eyes grew wide with horror.

"Oh my goodness!"

Then we all looked and saw inside the compartment that was the one Oliver Jackson had been staying in. There we saw that Mr. Jackson had hung himself.

Chapter 18

Benton arrived on the scene. To our discomfort we helped him take down the body. While we were busy he questioned Jean.

"So what were you doing walking around at this hour of the morning?"

"I had gone to see Len…"

"Len White?"

"Yes."

Benton looked at her with a bit of contempt.

"Now why would you need to see him at this hour?"

"We had dinner earlier but my stomach was upset. I didn't finish dinner and Len gave me something to calm me down. It worked but only for awhile. I went back to see if Len had more so I could get back to sleep. On the way back I fell against the door and it swung open and I saw…"

Jean started to tear up. I could tell Benton knew this part of the investigation was near an end but he still asked one more question.

"Did you see anyone leaving his room before you fell on the door?"

"No I didn't. Who would do such a thing like that to that poor man?"

"That's what I intend to find out. Maybe you should go to your room and lay down."

"I'll see you to your room." Said Micky.

I looked at Benton.

"Now do you believe Peter is innocent?"

"He's still a suspect but I am beginning to think your right. That's why I'll over look that he is once again out of his room. But get him back now. I'll have to check out with Len White about her alibi. It seems strange that her scream woke almost everyone on the train but him."

I looked towards the doorway. I could see a crowd had gathered and I didn't see Len in the group. However, I couldn't see everyone as some were around the corner. But if Len had been there wouldn't he have come in to comfort his friend Jean and help her to her room instead of Micky? Maybe what Oliver wanted to talk to me about had to do with Len or Jean.

Chapter 19

We met back in Mike and Peter's compartment. Davy joined us but Micky was still with Jean.

"Guys I think I should tell you that Oliver Jackson slipped me a note to meet him tonight."

I handed the note to Davy and Peter and Mike read the note over his shoulder.

"That explains why you were fully dressed when we woke up to the screaming," said Mike.

"Why didn't you tell us?" asked Davy.

"I didn't want to get your hopes up till I knew what he wanted. It may not have had anything to do with our investigation."

"Maybe he knew who the killer is," said Peter.

"It sure looks like that. Considering what Jean said there is a possibility it may be Len White."

"Why would he do it?" asked Peter.

"Maybe he really is having an affair with Jean," Davy said.

"Or maybe he just doesn't like being blackmailed." I said.

"Or both," said Mike.

At that moment the door opened and Micky came in the room.

"I thought I'd find you all in here."

"So how is Jean?" I asked.

"Calmer, I left her with Len."

Mike looked up at him.

"So he was awake."

"Well he had just woken up. He was yawning and still in his pajamas and wanted to know what all the noise was about. Why does it matter if he was awake?"

"Since he wasn't there after Jean screamed we thought he may have been the one who killed Mr. Jackson," I said.

"Well he has a motive to kill Mr. Pitts but why kill Jackson?"

I told him about the note that Oliver Jackson slipped me earlier.

"You think Jackson knew the identity of the killer and it may have been Len?"

"Or perhaps it was Jean."

"Oliver Jackson was a big man. How would she force him up on a chair or something so she could hang him?"

Peter looked at Micky with some concern.

"Maybe it was both of them." He said.

"Yeah," said Davy. "Maybe they approached Mr. Jackson together to explain themselves but he wouldn't listen so Len forced him on a chair and put his head through the noose."

"This all seems pretty slim evidence to me," said Mike.

"Still it has to be murder." I said. "I didn't see a suicide note did you?"

"No I didn't. So there still has to be a killer on the loose."

"Well some progress has been made," said Peter.

"What's that?" Asked Davy.

"Benton is starting to think I'm innocent."

"That's the only good think that came out of tonight."

With that we all decided to go to bed on a high note. Micky and Davy went to their compartment and Mike, Peter and I went to bed. But none of us slept well that night. I can't say for certain what kept Mike and Peter awake but for me it was the thought that the bodies were starting to pile up.

Chapter 20

After a sleepless night we all got up. We decided with Peter in the clear it seemed ok if we all went to the dining car for breakfast. As we walked there I noticed Peter trying not to smile.

"Peter no one will blame you for being happy."

"I know but it only came with the death of another man. That doesn't seem right."

"I know but everyone knows it wasn't you now. You were with all of us when the murder happened. So smile you! You don't have to go to prison."

As we walked into the car everyone seemed to be there. Benton was seated at a huge table with five chairs around it.

"I thought all of you would be here this morning." He said as he smiled at us.

"Have a seat and join me for breakfast."

As we all sat down Mike looked at Benton.

"You seem pretty happy for a man who had another murder happen on your watch."

"No one murders a man by hanging them anymore. I checked Jackson pockets after you left and I came up with this."

He passed Mike a note. Mike read it and passed it around to us all. I was the last to read it before I gave it back to Benton. It said…

"I cannot live with my guilt any longer. I was in some business deals with Pitts and White that didn't go as planned. Temper has always been a problem for me and it flared up and I killed them. I was going to confess but I can't live with going to prison. I have to end my life. This world would be better without me. Oliver Jackson"

"So Jackson was the killer?" Asked Davy.

"It looks that way."

"But I thought…ouch!" Said Peter.

"Sorry Pete." Said Micky.

The waiter came and we all placed our orders. Then there was small talk about Hollywood and showbiz. Benton wondered if there was a possibility that there could be a cop show about the railroad police. Micky said probably and asked if he had written a script. Benton said he had. He asked if Micky would look at it. Micky declined but said he should send it to some agents. Benton scowled at that answer. The waiter brought our meals. We said grace, I could tell Benton wasn't use to this custom but he went along with us, then we all ate in silence. After he was done Benton said his goodbye and left.

"Did anyone notice something odd about that note?" I whispered.

"Yeah the note was in a different handwriting then the one you have." Said Micky.

Peter looked at Micky.

"So that's why you kicked me."

"Sorry Pete. I didn't know if we should tell Benton about him wanting to meet Josh after reading that note."

"That means the killer is still on the train."

Mike looked around. No one seemed to notice our conversation. They were all involved in theirs or involved their meals.

"He could be in this car right now."

"Great! That means Len or Jean could still be involved," said Micky.

"Whoever it is they think they got away with it. With their guard down we can find out even more information."

I looked up and noticed Len White was eating with his cast mates from his show. At another table Jean Feldon was eating with Brandon Parks. They were laughing and smiling during their conversation.

"Well Jean seems to have put last night behind her," I said.

"Say I just thought of something. Len has the same last name as that guy that was killed the day before we left on this trip. I wonder if they were related?"

We all looked at Micky.

"How would I know?"

"Well you've known him for years," said Mike.

"That doesn't mean I know his whole family."

"Can you think of a discreet way to ask him?"

"Not right now but I'll think about it."

Chapter 21

It was later that day that the engineer found the problem and off we went. A sigh of relief seemed to echo through the whole train as we got underway. It was around that time that Micky went to the rear observation plat form to get some air. It was there that he told me he saw Len White. He told me how the meeting went.

"Hey Len! How's it going?"

"Hi Micky! Just wanted to get some air."

"Me too."

"I heard that Jackson fella was the guy who killed Pitts. "

"That's what I heard too."

"At least all of that's behind us."

"Len I don't know how to say this so I'm just going to come straight out and ask it. There was a businessman named Paul White who was killed before we left on this trip…."

"If you want to know if we were related the answer is yes. He was a distant cousin."

"I'm sorry if I brought back any bad memories."

"Don't be sorry. I didn't know him very well. Our families lost touch before I was born. His family came from Canada too but he was born in America. I didn't move to America till I was 32. That was to be in that movie where I met your Dad."

"That was Vendetta wasn't it?"

"Yeah! Did you see it?"

"No I was only 5 or 6 when it came out. Maybe I'll catch it on the late show sometime. "

"If you do you won't see me. I came here in 1946 to play the part of Brando. There were so many delays that by the time they got around to shooting the major scenes I was in I already had been cast in another movie. They recast the part with Hugo Haas. They even had to reshoot some of the minor scenes I was in. The only good things that came out of that movie was I got some film to show to other producers and my friendship with your Dad. Your family was more like family to me then Paul was."

"So you didn't feel any family ties to Paul."

"We'd have lunch sometimes and exchange Christmas cards but not really."

"So how did you feel when you were told Jackson was his killer too?"

"He was his killer? This is the first I heard about it. Who told you?"

Micky wasn't sure that he should tell him it was my editor who told us the killer was on board.

"I don't remember right now. Wait a minute I think that railroad cop Benton said it was in the suicide note."

"Well at least they found out who it was. If I hear from any family back in Canada I can tell them Justice was served."

They both went back to looking at the scenery. To Micky, Len seemed more relieved than before. Perhaps he was telling the truth when he said he didn't know Oliver Jackson was his cousin's killer. Still he could have been out for revenge on both Jackson and Pitts.

"To tell you the truth Mick I'm a little bit surprised it was him."

"Why?"

"Well I don't think he killed my cousin but I have seen him talking to Pitts in the past. They usually got along but once he got hold of his Dad's company they were always seen arguing. I was in the parking lot at the studio one night and I saw them talking. Pitts was trying to get in his car to leave but Parks wasn't letting him leave. It nearly came to blows. Parks had his hand on the car door and wasn't letting him close it. Pitts got out of the car and pushed him away. Parks pushed back. I rushed over and Parks was about to hit him but I got there in time to grab his arm so Parks didn't increase his chances of getting arrested for assault. But I guess I was wrong. I guess your friend Peter is relieved now that the spotlight is off of him."

"He is but isn't happy that it took another death to prove it."

"Well at least an innocent man won't be going to jail."

Micky thought that was true but now he thought an innocent man had died because he knew the truth. Len excused himself and left to go back to his compartment. Micky waited awhile so he wasn't seen rushing back to find the rest of us to tell us about their conversation.

Chapter 22

I was the last one that Micky found. I had been talking to Samantha Strong when Micky caught up and asked to talk in private. He actually dragged me back to his compartment where Davy, Mike and Peter were waiting. He told us he thought Len was innocent but Brandon Parks may be the guilty party.

"We all saw their conversation when they had breakfast that first morning on the train," Micky said.

"Yeah and it didn't look like they were having any fun," said Peter.

"But why would he have killed White?" asked Davy.

"When we can find out if and why he killed Pitts that should lead us to why he killed White," said Mike.

Davy looked at me.

"Not meaning to change the subject. But Micky said you were talking to Samantha."

"Getting worried Davy?"

"Well no not really," he said as he shuffled his feet.

"Come on I know you were talking to her before I was."

"Now who sounds worried?"

"It just came up in conversation."

"What was the conversation about?"

"I was just laying the groundwork in case I was assigned to interview her for the magazine when we got back."

"What groundwork for that would include me?"

"I asked her what it was like to be working in the same studio as you and the other stars on the network."

The others were growing impatient with us but it was Mike who finally spoke up.

"Will you two cut this out? We have more important things to discuss then your love lives."

We both looked like two children who had just been scolded by their Father. We answered in unison.

"Sorry Mike."

"What about Samantha?" asked Peter.

"Why?" asked Mike.

"Well someone had to kill those men. We know it wasn't really Oliver Jackson. It looks like Len White may be in the clear. She did have something against Pitts."

"But we don't know if she had anything against White," I said.

"Well someone has to ask her if she knew him," said Micky.

It was no surprise to anyone when Davy volunteered.

"You must really be scared of me," I said.

"Not in the way you mean. Your approach is everyone is a suspect."

"Everyone is."

"But everyone is also a victim. Pitts seemed to have hurt a lot of the people on this train. You need to approach them in a bit softer manner. "

"You won't mind if I talk to her about it too?"

Mike looked at me.

"Now we can't have both of you talking to her. No matter how soft the interrogation she'll feel that there is a target pinned on her."

Micky and Peter nodded in agreement.

"I hate to tell you this Josh but I think Davy should be the one to talk to her this time." said Micky

"As long as we get the real killer," I said.

Out of the corner of my eye I could see Davy get a little smile on his face. I really believed that it only mattered that we caught the real killer but I hated to have to give up Samantha to Davy.

Chapter 23

It was later that day that Davy saw Samantha. She was standing in the aisle talking to Jean Feldon. As Davy approached their conversation must have ended as Jean left. Samantha turned and was headed in the opposite direction of Jean. She looked up to see Davy coming her way.

"Hello David."

"Samantha, mind if I walk with you?

"Sure did you want to talk?"

"Have you been having a good day?"

"As well as can be. At least we don't have to worry about any more killings."

"Guess not. Did you know they are saying that Jackson killed two people?'

"Someone else on the train died?"

"No it was the day before the train left. Now what was his name...White, Paul White."

"Mr. White?"

"Did you know him? I'm sorry."

"Not well. He owned stock in the network. He was Len White's cousin and sometimes he would stop and take Len to lunch."

"But you and Len aren't on the same show. How did you see him?"

"Now don't play dumb Davy. You've been in this business long enough to know that people who own a lot of stock in networks will drop by the studios sometimes when they are in town to see how the business is being run. When you're the #3 network they stop by more often. So Paul White was there a lot and every time he took Len to lunch. Your show and mine win their time slots most of the time so they aren't too worried about us. The one they really love is Len's show. The Ranchers is the only show they have in the top ten every year. Len is treated like royalty and by extension so is his cousin Paul."

"I know Garfield Pitts came on to you. Did Paul White?"

"No he was a perfect gentleman. The only thing he thought he was bothering me with was when he asked me for an autograph for his granddaughter. I told him it was no bother and I gave him an autographed photo. Why all the questions if there was no other murder on the train? Davy, tell me the truth. Oliver Jackson was the real killer wasn't he?"

"We're hoping he was but to be careful were just asking some follow up questions."

"I think you're being a little more than cautious but I'll let it go."

With that Samantha decided to end the conversation. She said goodbye to Davy and gave him a kiss on the cheek. As

Davy came around the corner he saw me leaning against the wall and he jumped a little because of the surprise.

"Josh! I didn't know you were there."

"I know you didn't hot lips."

"What do you mean? She just kissed me on the cheek."

"I also saw you pucker up and lean in to kiss her on the lips. She backed off and kissed you on the cheek."

"It just heightens the tension. It makes it even better when we finally do go on that date and share our first real kiss."

"Either way I didn't hear the whole conversation. So what did you find out?"

"Well I don't think she knew Paul White that well and I don't think she did anything to him. But I wonder if Len didn't know his cousin better than we thought. From what she says they had lunch together a lot."

"It could just be something innocent. You know just catching up on family."

"Or it could be they were making plans for something."

"But what could they have been planning that could have led to three men dying?"

"I don't know. Has anyone talked to Brandon Parks?"

"I'm not sure. Why?"

"Well he's a Network executive on the train and Pitts and White would have talked to him on some of their visits. He may know more about what is going on. As a matter of fact I think you should talk to him."

"Why me?"

"Well since I'm in show business some of the questions I asked, Samantha saw through. She is very smart and Parks is probably smarter. He'll know that I already have the answers to the questions I ask. But he may not suspect it from you."

"Ok I'll talk to him."

After that Davy and I parted ways. I decided to look for Parks. I went to his room but there was no answer when I knocked. I didn't find him in the dining car and everyone I asked didn't know where he was. After awhile I just gave up thinking when I went to his room he was probably asleep or something and didn't hear the knock. It had been awhile since I worked on the article so I went back to the compartment and started working on it.

After awhile I got sleepy. It had been a long day and I laid down on Peter's lower berth. I just meant to rest but next thing I know I was waking up. I saw Peter on my cot. I could tell Mike was in the upper berth and noticed that the clock said one o'clock.

"That's odd," I thought.

I looked out the window and it was dark. I turned and looked again at Peter and saw he was in his pajamas. I looked to the upper berth and Mike was also dressed for bed and sleeping.

I thought to myself, "I can't believe that I was so tired that I didn't hear them come in or hear Mike practically climb over me to get to his bed. I'm up so much in the wee hours of the evening that by the time this trip is over I'll have my days and nights mixed up."

I was wide awake so I quietly left the room and went to the dining car. I was thirsty but there wasn't anyone there to get a drink from. But I did see Brandon Parks sitting at a table. There was a full 16 oz. bottle of Coke and a glass of ice in front of him.

"Mr. Adams," he said, "Have a seat. I hear you've been looking for me. If you're wondering where I was I was probably sending a wire to Clarksville to tell them why we were delayed but are now on our way."

I sat down. He poured half the soft drink in the glass and slid the half empty bottle to me.

"I got here a few minutes ago just before they closed down. I tried to get something stronger than a soft drink but all I could coax out of them was this. You won't be able to get anything to drink for a few hours so you can have half the bottle."

"Thanks I was thirsty."

"You're welcome but I don't think you were looking for me this afternoon because you wanted a free soft drink."

"You're right. I wanted to ask you about how you knew Paul White."

"Well I knew him from stockholder meetings as he held stock in the network. He would drop by from time to time to meet with me. Why do you need to know that?"

"It would seem that Pitts and White were killed by the same person."

"I do remember reading in the paper before we left that he had died. But Jackson confessed to killing Pitts. So isn't this questioning a bit after the fact?"

With that question I hesitated. I tried to think of how to answer him but couldn't think of another way. So I decided to be honest.

"You're an intelligent man Mr. Parks. I won't insult that intelligence by trying to sound dumb or make up a story. I don't think that Oliver Jackson was the killer. I think he knew who the killer was."

"You think the real killer got to him and made it look like he was the murderer?"

"Yes I do."

"What makes you believe this?"

"I'd rather not say till I have concrete proof who the real killer is."

"You don't think I'm the killer do you?"

"Not at the moment. I wouldn't be telling you this if I did."

"You're brutally honest I'll say that for you."

"I hope I can rely on your discretion."

"No one will find out because of me."

"What were you usually talking about with White on his visits?"

"Not much with White. He usually just stopped by to say hello, check on his investments and have lunch with his cousin Len. "

"What about Jackson? I understand he would stop by the network sometimes too."

"Oliver was all business. He wanted to increase his involvement in the network."

"He was involved in the running of the network! Isn't that unheard of for a stockholder?"

"Unless you're the majority stockholder it is. He kept telling me he thought we should have call in shows for people to buy things from us on TV. It was in interesting idea but why would people want to pay to have an item shipped to them. They can just go to their local department store and buy it there. It would save them the cost of shipping. We would have to charge even more to put in the phone lines from around the country and hire the people to do the show and man the telephones. It wasn't cost effective. Jokes were being told about him and when he came people avoided him. In truth I felt sorry for him. "

"Why?"

"He had ambition but not the business sense to bring it about. Sometimes it's good to not know what you're doing. But usually it isn't. In his case he could have brought down the whole network with that idea. Garfield Pitts did have business sense but didn't seem to care if the network was destroyed."

"What do you mean?"

"Pitts hated TV. He always said it didn't take brain power to watch something happen. But his Dad owned and ran the company so there was nothing he could do. Then his Dad retired and left the business to him. Pitts always felt that the railroad was the way to make money. He hated owning stock in a television network so much that he was willing to sell it cheap. "

"That first morning on the train I saw you and him talking. It kind of got out of hand."

"We were talking about him selling the stock. Selling it so low it would have brought down the price of the network. It would have cost jobs because we would have to let some people go. I tried to change his mind but all he would say is he had a capable person in mind for it. It just makes me mad when others don't care about other people's lives."

With that said I just sat there and took a drink of my soft drink. I guess he felt safe telling me his anger to Pitts. But if he had been angry with White about something I would have now suspected him as the murderer.

Chapter 24

After my talk with Parks I went back to the compartment. Peter and Mike were still asleep. I quietly made my way to the lower berth to lie down. I looked at the clock and could barely see it in the darkness but it looked like it was 2:30 in the morning. I lay there for a long time and tossed and turned but I must have fallen asleep sometime because the next thing I remember was hearing Mike's feet hit the floor next to me. I turned over then sat up and put my feet on the floor too. Mike looked at me and yawned. Then he smiled.

"Morning sleepyhead," he said.

"Morning."

"Nothing like a 14 hour nap is there?"

"I didn't sleep the entire 14 hours. I went out around one in the morning to the Dining car and talked to Parks who was having trouble sleeping. Why didn't you guys wake me?"

Peter had just awoken. He looked at me.

"We tried to around dinner time but you must have just gotten to sleep and just waved us off."

Hearing the term dinner time made me realize I hadn't eaten since lunch yesterday and was hungry. That drink I had around one in the morning must have filled me up enough that I didn't feel the hunger than but I was starving now.

"Sorry about that Pete and for taking your bed."

"That's ok. It wasn't a problem."

The three of us quickly washed up and changed clothes. Mike said I didn't have to but I told him I didn't want that chic slept in his clothes look.

We made our way to the Dining car. Not long after we got there Micky and Davy came in. The car was empty except for the five of us.

"This is a first," said Peter.

"What is?" I asked.

"The performers are up before the businessmen."

Since we were alone I quickly told them of the conversation I had with Brandon Parks.

"So he thought Pitts could have put employees out of work," said Mike.

"Maybe even take the whole network under," said Davy.

"I told him I didn't think he was the killer but after hearing his side I was starting to wonder."

"I don't think he did it," said Peter.

"Neither do I," said Micky.

"Why not?"

"Well it could hurt the network like he said if the stock was sold cheaply. Maybe take the network down. But one thing that would do it even faster was if a network executive was arrested for murder," answered Micky.

We all looked to Peter to see why he thought Parks was innocent. Peter seemed puzzled as to why we were looking at him. Finally he realized why and he pointed to Micky.

"What he said."

We all laughed. Just then the waiter came to take our order. As we placed our food orders the other travelers came in.

Chapter 25

Not long after breakfast Micky said he and Peter went to the back observation deck and watched as the scenery passed by.

"I don't believe Parks was the killer and can't believe Jackson actually thought people would call up a TV network to buy things," said Micky.

"Neither can I. You can just go to a shopping mall and buy what you want," said Peter.

"Still, people do shop by mail from those catalogues."

"Yeah and people did call in to those radio quiz programs. Maybe he was on to something."

Just then Jake Pitts opened the door. He was holding his Grandfather by the arm as he helped his steady him as they came out on the deck.

"Hey Peter!"

"Hey…eh…eh…"

"Jake, I don't think I gave you my name when he met."

"I understand. You were very upset that your Dad died. Micky this is Mr. Pitts' son and..."

"Oh! This is my Grandfather."

Micky shook hands with Jake and his Grandfather.

"Sorry about your son," he said as he looked at Pitts Sr.

"Thank you. At least everyone now knows that your friend here didn't do it."

"That is the one good thing to come out of it. Well there isn't much room out here for four people so we'll leave you two alone," said Micky as he placed his hand on the doorknob.

Pitts Sr. placed his hand on Peter's right arm. Peter stopped.

"If you don't mind son I'd like you to stay and talk for awhile."

Peter looks towards Micky.

"I'll let the guys know where you are Pete. It was nice meeting you both."

The door closes behind Micky. For awhile the three men stand looking at the countryside without saying a word. Peter wonders what Mr. Pitts wants but doesn't know if it would be polite for him to speak first. Finally the older gentleman speaks.

"You know you're program is my Grandson's favorite. He makes sure he is home in time to see it every week."

"That's nice."

"As a matter of fact you're his favorite actor on the show."

"That's true," said Jake.

"He actually convinced me once to watch the show when he was at my house. I believe it was when one of you had written a song that you were trying to sell. I could see why you're his favorite."

"I remember that one. But that episode was about Mike not me."

"I know but it was when you tried to cheer him up by complimenting him on his posture that made me think of Jake. That's something that he would have done if he couldn't think of a joke to cheer up a friend. Since then I have watched the show from time to time and when I see you I feel like I'm watching Jake. You make me feel closer to him when he isn't there."

Peter is touched. He almost wants to cry but he holds it back. Just like on that episode Peter doesn't know what to say. He puts his hand on the older man's shoulder and gives him a small squeeze as his way of saying you're welcome.

"Because of the happiness that you have brought us I would like to make up for you the problem that my family has caused you."

"You haven't caused me any problem. I tripped into this situation. I could have avoided this situation if I had just been more careful where I stepped or if I just stayed in my compartment."

"That may be. But if my son had not gotten himself into a situation, then you wouldn't have either. So what can I do for you?"

"Nothing, I'm just happy that everyone now knows I didn't do it."

"I know you didn't but I hope you find the real killer soon."

Peter is stunned. This man somehow knows Oliver Jackson wasn't the killer. But how? Has he been investigating it himself?

"Mr. Jackson confessed in his suicide note. Why do you think he didn't do it?"

"I've known Oliver Jackson for years. We've done business together many times. He has done a lot of things and made many bad decisions. No matter how regretful he feels he has never talked of suicide."

"But this was probably too big for him to handle."

"I still think that Jackson is innocent. He just was not the suicidal type. He was many things but he was not a coward. He always faced adversity head on. He even got a medal for his actions in the Korean War."

The older Pitts looked at his grandson.

"I'm getting a little cold out here. Jake, please take me back. Peter if there is anything I can do for you just let me know."

With that they left. Peter turned to look down the tracks to think about this conversation.

Chapter 26

Later that morning Peter met Mike in their compartment. He told him of the conversation that he had with Mr. Pitts Sr.

"Well he seems to be an intelligent man. No wonder the railroad has thrived till now," said Mike.

"I know and I was very touched at how he said that he enjoyed my work. Did anyone ever say anything about Mr. Jackson being in the Korean War?"

"No one said anything to me."

"Let's find the other guys to see if they heard anything."

They eventually found Davy and me talking to Samantha Strong. Samantha noticed them arriving before we did.

"Hello Mike. Peter it's nice to see you. I'm so happy to know you're not a suspect. I must say you've held up quite well under the scrutiny."

"Thanks Samantha. I didn't really have much choice."

"We wanted to ask you guys a question. Did anyone tell you anything about Oliver Jackson being a Korean War hero?" asked Mike.

"I barely knew Mr. Jackson. I didn't know anything about him being in the service," said Samantha.

"No one ever told me about his war record," I said.

"Me neither," said Davy.

"Why do you need to know about that?" asked Samantha.

Mike looked as if he wondered if he should tell her that we know Oliver Jackson is not the real killer. Before he could answer her Davy did.

"We promised to find out some things for the obituary."

"That's right and I figured at his age, if he was in the service, he was probably in the Korean War."

"That may be but why did you ask if he was a hero?"

"Well it would make a better story if he was," I said.

She had this annoyed look on her face. I don't think she really believed us but she didn't have any reason to not believe us either.

"Ok, well I better go and wire my manager to see if he has any jobs for me."

As she left her last comment rang a bell with me. I hadn't heard from my editor in awhile. I knew I would have to check in with him soon if I didn't hear from him first.

"Ok guys, she's gone now. Why do you need to know about Jackson's military record?" asked Davy.

"Pitts Sr. told me he knew that Jackson was a hero in the Korean War," said Peter.

"He suspects that he wasn't the real killer because of that," added Mike.

"He said he was the kind of guy who faced his problems," said Peter.

"I was thinking about contacting my editor later. I can ask him to see if he can find anything out about this."

"Has he contacted you about any more info on the other passengers?" asked Mike.

"No that's why I may have to contact him soon."

"Has anyone seen Micky? Maybe he knows more about this," said Davy.

Unknown to us at that time Micky was with Benton.

Micky was walking down the aisle of the train. Suddenly he heard someone walking behind him. Not unusual with the amount of people on board. But the footsteps were heavy as well as the breathing he heard coming from the person.

"Hey Dolenz, what's going on?"

"Not much Benton how have you been?"

"I've been able to take it a little easier since the killer is no longer on board."

Micky wanted to tell him about the other note but decided to wait till they all thought it was the right time.

"I guess you have."

"How's the rest of your trip been?"

"I've had a perfectly wonderful trip. But this wasn't it."

"Say Benton did you know any of the passengers before this trip?"

"I knew the Pitts family but just from seeing them at the train station from time to time. The rest I only knew from when I saw them on TV."

"Did you know Oliver Jackson?"

"No! Why are you asking me these questions?"

"I'm just trying to figure things out in my head."

"If you're trying to still figure out who the killer is I already told you. It was Jackson. You don't need to look for any more suspects."

"I know I just want to have it all make some sense to me."

Just then Mike, Peter and Davy found Micky. I was told all of this as I had gone to wire my editor the part of the story that I had up to that point and to ask if he could find more information on Oliver Jackson.

"Hey Mick!" called Mike.

"Hey guys."

"We have been looking all over this train for you. Did anyone tell you if Jackson was in the Korean War?" blurted Peter.

"No why would they?"

"Yeah what would that have to do with anything?" quizzed Benton.

The three new Monkees on the scene all looked at each other.

"You think we should tell him?" asked Peter.

"I think we should. The more people to look into this the quicker we'll find the answers," said Davy.

Mike looked at Benton and told him of the other note we had and how it didn't have the same handwriting as the one he showed us. He also told him what Mr. Pitts told Peter and how all of this may prove that Oliver Jackson may not be the real killer.

"Why didn't you tell me till now? The real killer may have jumped off the train by now."

"While it was still moving?" asked Davy.

Benton fumed when he looked at him.

"It could happen," he said quietly.

Benton then looked at Micky.

"So much for a peaceful second half of the ride. I'll keep my eyes open and keep you informed if I find anything. Which is more than what I can say you did for me."

"We didn't want to tip our hand till we had more concrete evidence," said Mike.

"If he won a medal for bravery in the war then that may prove he wouldn't kill himself," said Davy.

"I suppose so." Answered Benton.

Benton turned to start to leave. Peter stopped him. Benton turned back and looked at Peter.

"What do you want kid?"

"This doesn't mean I'm a suspect again does it?"

"No! You were with them when Jackson was killed. It couldn't have been you. Now look I am very upset with the four…did Adams know about this?"

"He's the one who got the note."

"Ok the five of you. Stay clear of me unless you have something to share."

With that he turned and walked away.

"I guess we should have told him earlier," said Micky.

"At least we have another pair of eyes and ears still looking into this," said Mike.

"That's not all," said Peter.

"What else is there?" asked Davy.

"At least I'm still not a suspect," said a beaming Peter.

With that good news they all smiled.

Chapter 27

Later I ran in to Micky, who it turned out had just left the others but I didn't know that at that moment.

"Micky! Where have you been? The others were looking for you."

"They found me. I was talking to Benton. "

"About what?"

"Nothing much at the time. Mostly how he was able to take it easier now that the killer was caught."

"Did they tell you what Peter found out?"

"Yeah and since Benton was there we also told him about the note that you had."

I didn't care to hear that. I still thought it was something we should have kept to ourselves.

"I wish we could have kept that to ourselves but I guess that couldn't be helped since he was there when they told you."

"He wasn't too happy that we had a clue we kept from him."

"Well he does make his living doing this, catching criminals and all."

"So what were you doing at that time?"

"I was wiring my editor."

"Did he get back to you about what you asked him earlier?"

"No he hasn't I am curious as to why but he does have other stories to work on."

"So what did you tell him?"

"Well I did get him some of the article that I was working on. I also asked him to see if he can find out anymore on Oliver Jackson. I told him of him being a Korean War vet and I also asked him of reasons why there may be broken pieces of glass at the scene and why would the killer take them."

"I hope word doesn't get out that we still suspect that the real killer is still on board," whispered Micky.

"We've already put it out there."

"What do you mean?"

"I told Parks and now you've told Benton."

"Yeah a few more and half the train will know."

"Well if they keep their eyes open and their mouths shut that's at least two more detectives on the lookout."

"I just hope no one else dies before we get to Clarksville."

Chapter 28

Later that night I saw Sgt. Benton. He was having a cup of coffee in the dining car. I approached him at his table.

"Benton how are you?"

"Not bad just a little tired. I just stopped to get a little something to pick me up. Thanks to you and your friends I have to stay on 24 hour alert now."

"Sorry we didn't tell you earlier."

"Just keep me in the loop on anything else you find. I was actually going to Pitts car in a minute to talk to him. You want to tag along?"

"Sure."

Benton put down his now empty cup and stood up from his seat. Without a word between us we walked almost the entire length of the train. Soon we approached the private car of Harrison Pitts Sr. As we did I saw Brandon Parks leaving the car.

"Well Sgt. Benton and Mr. Adams. How nice to see you again."

"Hi!" said Benton.

"Hello Mr. Parks. Do you mind if I ask why you were in with Mr. Pitts?"

"Not at all. We were just talking some business."

"I didn't think he ran the business anymore." Said Benton.

"Well that's the sixty four thousand dollar question now isn't it? Who is running Pitts inc.? Anyway I'll see you later."

With that he left and Benton knocked on the door.

"Come in," said Pitts.

We entered a car that you could almost live in. It was decorated in an art deco style and the back half of the car was set up like a bedroom. The front part that we had now entered was set as an office. It was in this part of the car that Henderson Pitts Sr. was seated in behind his desk. He slowly rose to his feet.

"Well Sgt. Benton and Mister....oh I know I've seen you before with those Mercies, I mean Monkees.

"That's ok Mr. Pitts. I don't think we've been formally introduce. My name is Joshua Adams."

"Well it's nice to finally meet you Mr. Adams. Now how can I be of service to you two gentlemen?"

"Actually I was the one who wanted to see you Mr. Pitts. I just asked Mr. Adams if he wanted to tag along. I understand that you don't think Oliver Jackson is the one who killed your boy. Mind if I ask why?"

"Not at all. I knew him for many years. Since he was discharged from the Army. I believe it was 1953. He needed a job but I wasn't able to hire him. Normally that would be the end of it but I saw that he had a medal for bravery. I couldn't ignore that and made a few phone calls that helped him get a job. Later he went into the plastics business. He made a few smart decisions and that made him a fairly wealthy businessman."

"I still don't understand."

"What don't you understand?"

"None of that tells why you think he was innocent."

"But all of it does Sgt. you see a smart man would see how suicide is permanent answer to temporary problems. Still he could be a coward and not want to face those problems and kill himself. On the other hand a man may not be very intelligent but can be brave and want to face those same problems and accept what his punishment will be. Mr. Jackson was smart and brave. He would not kill himself. I'm sure you've met a few men like this in your life Sgt. Benton."

"What do you mean by that?"

"Just being in your line of work and involved in other activities."

"That still doesn't explain why you think he is innocent. It only means you don't think he would kill himself."

"But it does explain it. If he didn't kill himself then…"

"…he had to be murdered," I said.

"Correct Mr. Adams. Who would have wanted Jackson dead but the real killer? Why I don't know. Maybe there was a connection to him and my son I don't know about or maybe he discovered the real identity of the killer. Either way he…"

Mr. Pitts doubled over and sat down once more behind his desk. He grabbed his chest. He then opened his left hand desk drawer. He took out a bottle of capsules. He opened the bottle and took out one and swallowed the pill.

"Are you all right?" Benton and I asked in unison.

"I'll be ok. I sometimes forget to take my heart medicine and that was a reminder that it was pill time. Anyway, those are my reasons for thinking Oliver Jackson is innocent. Is there anything else Private Benton?"

"Nothing more from me Mr. Pitts. I just wanted to make sure what your reasoning was. Also it's SGT. Benton not Private." Said Benton

"I'm sorry Sgt. My memory isn't what it used to be."

"Well I'm fine too sir. You take care of yourself now," I said as we both left.

"I will and you two gentlemen do the same." Said Mr. Pitts as we closed the door behind us.

"Ok what was all that about?" I asked.

"I just wanted to make sure he had a good reason for suspecting that he wasn't the killer," said Benton.

"We told you that we had a note in a different handwriting that Jackson slipped in my pocket. That alone should be enough."

"You never showed me the note."

I had the note in my pocket and took it out. I held it out to Benton. He started to take it but I pulled it away at the last minute.

"I'd like to hold on to it."

"It's evidence."

"I know but you really won't need it till we get off the train. I'll give it to you then."

Benton just glared at me but seeing it wasn't having any effect he took a closer look at the note.

"Well it is a different handwriting. Still we only have your word it came from Jackson. But for now that is good enough."

"Well that's true I suppose."

As we continued our walk I could detect a sweet smell in the air. I then looked over at Benton. He had a wrapper in his hand and I could hear him chewing on something.

"What are you eating?"

"Some hard candy. I have a sweet tooth. Want a piece?"

"No thanks. I just smelled something sweet and was wondering where it was coming from."

We walked through the rest of the cars till we were passing Samantha Strong's compartment.

"Josh I was just coming to find you or Davy. Can you help me?"

I would give anything to be with Samantha and to score points with her instead of Davy was an added plus.

"Sure, will you excuse me Sgt. Benton?"

"Of course." He said.

Benton continued walking down the aisle. Sam grabbed my right arm and nearly pulled me off my feet as we went into her compartment.

"I just got a wire from my Manager. It seems they are doing a new version of Romeo and Juliet. He has arranged for me to audition when we finish shooting some episodes for next season."

"What do you mean shooting episodes for next season? Well the scripts I've been reading to shoot when I get back won't be aired till late August or early September. We do that so we have a jump on the next season. Sometimes the other networks are still airing reruns then and new viewers watch us since we have new episodes on. "

"That makes sense."

"I hope I get the part. I hear Paul McCartney may be playing Romeo. He is so dreamy."

Great more competition from England, I thought to myself.

"What can I help with?"

"I was hoping you could read the part of Romeo with me in the script I was sent."

We read the script and Samantha was very good. I, on the other hand, showed why I was a writer. Still all was going well till we got to the balcony scene. Romeo had the biggest part and to my surprise and I am sure Samantha's I did pretty well. Then she read her lines.

"'Tis but thy name that is my enemy. Thou art thyself, though not a Montague. What's Montague? It is nor hand, nor foot, Nor arm, nor face. O, be some other name Belonging to a man. What's in a name? That which we call a rose by any other word would smell as sweet. So Romeo would, were he not Romeo called, Retain that dear perfection which he owes without that title. Romeo, doff thy name; And for thy name, which is no part of thee, Take all myself."

We were both sitting on the couch and with that last line Samantha had leaned forward. Her bright red lips were pursed and I didn't see a trace of lipstick on them. I just sat there stunned at her beauty as her long blond hair flowed down. I looked into her bright blue eyes and said my line.

"I take thee at thy word."

With that I leaned forward and kissed her on the lips. She pulled back and looked at me in surprise. Then she stuttered out her next line.

"Wh…Wh…What man art thou, that, thus be screened in night?"

With that said she kissed me. Then we held hands and smiled. She put my arm over her shoulders and we sat back and read the rest of the script out loud for the rest of the time.

Chapter 29

Later I was in the compartment reading a book that I brought with me. It was getting dark and I was trying to make myself sleepy so I wouldn't be up all night. Suddenly there was a knock at the door. I opened the door and Davy barged in.

"YOU KISSED HER!" He shouted.

"Kissed who?" I asked trying to act like it happened so often I wasn't sure who he was talking about.

"Don't play with me you know who."

"If you mean Samantha, well yes. I was in the moment."

"Don't think that means she likes you more than she does me."

"Actually I think it does since she kissed me back. How did you find out anyway?"

"I was just with her."

"How did I, kissing her, come up in conversation?"

"That's not important. I just…"

"You just thought you would get a kiss before me."

"Maybe she doesn't have as good a taste as I thought."

Just then Mike barged into the room.

"There you two are we've been looking for you."

"I've been here for at least a half an hour," I said.

"What did you need us for?" Asked Davy.

"It's Mr. Pitts Sr. He's dead."

I fell into the chair behind me. Davy hung his head in sorrow.

"How?" I asked. "I only saw him a few hours ago and he seemed fine."

"I don't know yet," said Mike. "A bunch of us are meeting with Jake and his Uncle in the Dining car. We thought you two would want to be there."

The three of us made our way through the cars. When we got near the Dining car Micky saw us coming through the window. He opened the door for us.

"Hey Mick," Mike whispered.

"Hey, where did you find them?"

"In my compartment the second time I looked."

When I heard that I knew Mr. Pitts had to have died at least over a half an hour ago.

"How did he die?" I asked.

"I heard it was a heart attack."

"He wasn't murdered?"

"Doesn't look like it. That's first on this trip." Said Micky.

The care was filled with passengers of the train. Reporters from the press car, who had been at the previous killings, were there too. At the other times Benton prevented the reporters from taking pictures but tonight flash bulbs were practically lighting up the car. Between flashes I looked at the end of the car. There I saw Jake and his Uncle with Brandon Parks. He had his hand on Jake's shoulder.

"Is Parks trying to comfort them?" asked Mike.

By now Peter, who had been up front and offered his condolences to the family had made his way back to us.

"Yeah, and if he looks shaken it's probably because he found the body," he said in answer to Mike's question.

I could see Jake, his Uncle and Parks kind of huddle together. Then they turned to the press. Jake and his Uncle sat down. Parks shook off his look of shock and took center stage.

"The Pitts family is still in a bit of shock at the death of their beloved Father and Grandfather. With the death of two family members and a business associate this has been a very harrowing trip for them. It has taken a lot of strength for them to deal with all of this but there strength is almost gone and I have been asked to act as spokesman for the family.

I was with Henderson Pitts Sr. couple of time earlier today. We were talking about the future of the network. The first time was in his private car and when I left he was being visited by reporter Joshua Adams and Sgt. Benton. Later we had something to eat in this very car. He had to leave as he had some chest pains. Some of you may not know this but he has been in bad health for some time now. He required constant medication for his heart. But he was a bit absent minded and sometimes would forget to bring his pills with him. This was one of those times. He went back to get his pills. He hadn't come back for awhile so I went to check on him. I knocked but there was no answer. The door was unlocked so I went in. I found him lying on the floor behind his desk. I tried to revive him but it was too late. I guess he didn't get to his medicine in time. Now please excuse us there will be no questions."

With all that said Parks helped the remaining members of the Pitts family out the nearest door. The reporters then turned their attention to Sgt. Benton. Parks may have said no more questions but Benton was now fair game as the questions came at a fast and furious pace. The most that were repeated where when did Benton find out and if he suspected foul play. While not accustomed to the spotlight Benton handled himself very well.

"When did you find out about his death Sgt. Benton?

"Almost as soon as Mr. Parks did. I was one of the first he told."

"Do you suspect it was murder?"

"He already told you how it happened. He was not a young man and not in good health. He just didn't get his medicine in time."

With that we left the car. We walked back to our compartment.

"This doesn't seem right," I said.

"What do you mean?" asked Peter.

133

"Pitts Sr. was convinced that the real killer was still on the train and that Oliver Jackson may have been killed because he knew something."

"Now he is also dead." Said Davy.

"This should make anyone a believer that the killer is still at large." Said Micky.

"But it wasn't murder this time." Said Mike.

"I still think it has something to do with the previous murders," I said.

Chapter 30

Soon we were near our compartments. As we entered the next car there was a Porter at the far end.

"Mr. Adams!" he shouted.

His paced quickened as the five of us continued walking toward him.

"I was just at your compartment Mr. Adams but you weren't there."

"No we were in the other car with the reporters."

"Well there was a wire that came for you. It was still coming over when I was told to come and get you."

"It was still coming over! That must be a long message."

"It sure is. You can come with me."

I bid the guy's farewell and was off to the communication car. Peter told me what happened later while I was gone. They were all back at Mike and Peter's compartment when a knock came on the door.

"Who is it?" asked Mike.

"It's Benton!"

Peter opened the door.

"Come on in."

"Thanks, I see that most of you are here so I guess it isn't too late for me to be calling on you. So what do you four think of the current death on this train?"

"We were discussing that," said Mike.

"It seems pretty odd to us," said Micky.

"That's what I thought too," said Benton.

"But if it was murder who could have done it?" asked Davy.

"I don't know. We may be back at square one," said Benton.

"Well Parks was the last one to see him," said Mike.

"Yeah! He was also upset that a stock sale would make the network almost worthless," said Peter.

"Having a change of heart about him Pete?" asked Davy.

"Not really. I'm just trying to keep an open mind."

"Of course he was around his Grandson Jake a lot," said Micky.

"He did stand to inherit it all," said Mike.

"See what I mean? This is one of the most puzzling cases of my career," said Benton.

"Especially since the most puzzling cases so far have been trying to keep bums off the train," said Micky.

Benton turned to Micky and gave him a mean look that faded quickly.

"Mr. Dolenz! It is true that is what the bulk of my work has consisted of but there is a lot more to policing the railroad then that."

"Now simmer down there pardner. Sometimes Micky speaks before thinks," said Mike

"That's true. I didn't mean anything by it. Thanks for defending me. At least I think I should thank you for it," said Micky.

"I'm sorry kid. It's just that some people don't think a railroad cop is a real policeman," said Benton. "I get a little bit touchy about it sometimes."

After that Benton left. It was much later that night when I got back. Davy and Micky had already gone back to their compartment and Peter and Mike were fast asleep. I had an idea but didn't want to wake them. I went over to a table and sat down and wrote some notes. I then left a note on my cot. I then went and slipped a note under Micky and Davy's door. Then I went and slipped others under the doors of the other passengers. Then I went to the Dining car. I was still keyed up so it was easy to stay up and wait.

Dawn was breaking. The cooks and waiters were all in the kitchen getting ready for breakfast. Mike, Davy, Micky and Peter came in on the far end of the car. They quickly made their way to me on the opposite end.

"Ok man what's with all they mystery?" asked Mike.

"Haven't we had enough of that on this trip?" asked Davy.

"So why did you want to meet us here at dawn?" asked Micky.

"Sit down boys and we can talk."

As they sat a waiter entered the car with five glasses of orange juice.

"Have a drink guys. In about an hour you may all need your strength."

Chapter 31

I had just read the wire that I had gotten from my editor last night. We were still in the middle of discussing it when the first of our "guest" arrived. It was Sgt. Benton.

"What's the meaning of this Adams? This note invited me to a meeting at breakfast saying that the killer would be revealed today."

"Sorry about that Benton. I only figured it out late last night. Otherwise I would have told you earlier. I didn't want to wake anyone up if they were finally getting a good night sleep on this trip since it was our last night before we arrived."

I looked back to the end of the car. I could see the others were starting to arrive. They all had one of my notes in hand and were asking each other about its meaning.

"I'm afraid I don't have time to go into it now Benton. Just follow my lead."

They all took their seats in the same manner they had been on this whole trip. Business men on one side of the car and the performers on the other.

Parks was sitting at a table with Jake Pitts and his Uncle. Len White was sitting with his cast mates of "The Ranchers" and at the table next to them were seated some actresses. Among them at the table were Samantha Strong and Jean Feldon. With no more room at our table Benton took a seat alone at the table in the corner. He was keeping an eye on the others to see any signs of guilt and another eye on me since he had no idea what I was up to. All was now quiet till Brandon Parks stood up.

"Well Mr. Adams. It seems you have all of our attention with your notes for this early morning meeting. Why don't you just tell us who this killer is and have Sgt. Benton arrest him or her?"

"I will arrest them once he tells me who it is and why he suspects them," said Benton.

As Parks sat down I stood up. I walked to the center of the car.

"I won't bore you with all saying that one of you is a killer. We all know that by now. What some of you don't know is the number of deaths that have happened at the hands of this person. How many would you say they had killed?"

Numbers started flying at me. Mostly I heard people say the killer only murdered one person. Others said two if you count his suicide since most of the passengers still believed that Oliver Jackson was the killer. I looked at Brandon Parks.

"All good educated guesses but all are wrong. How many would you venture a guess at Mr. Parks?" I asked.

Brandon Parks smiled. He thought he had the answer and said it loudly and proudly.

"Three Mr. Adams. Two on the train and one the day before we left."

"That is very close Mr. Parks."

Parks looked angry. He was a prideful man and I had just made him look foolish.

"What do you mean close? We talked about this earlier. Paul White was killed earlier the day the train left. Pitts was killed later and you said Jackson was killed because he knew who the killer was. That's three."

"But you're leaving out Henderson Pitts Sr."

"He wasn't murdered. He died of a heart attack before he got his medicine."

"Maybe he did but let's assume that he didn't. We need to know who had a motive to kill all four men. Almost all of you had a reason to kill Garfield Pitts. First there is Samantha Strong. Garfield Pitts loved his women. He came on to Miss Strong but she kept turning down his advances. To get back at her he pulled some strings that took away any chance she had at a movie career. But why would she kill Paul White, Oliver Jackson or Henderson Pitts Sr.? None of them ever came on to her or tried to take away her career. "

Out of the corner of my eye I could see Samantha. When I first mentioned her name she seemed tense. Once I said she had no reason to kill the others she seemed to relax.

"Next we have Jean Feldon. Jean is an up and coming actress in her own sit-com. Like Samantha, she too was hit on by Garfield Pitts. Also like Samantha she kept turning him down. Being friends with Len White she confided in him. He gave her some fatherly advice but that didn't work out. Pitts started a rumor that she and Len were having an affair. The rumor was not true and it didn't hurt Len's career or family life but it almost destroyed Jean's. But what did she have against Paul White, Oliver Jackson or Henderson Pitts Sr. Nothing. "

"What about your friend Tork?" asked one of the actresses at Jean's table.

"Yes Peter was the first suspect. He did have a misunderstanding with Garfield Pitts before getting on the train and was in the neighborhood at the time Paul White was murdered. He had seen them both around the studios but was cleared because he was still being watched when Oliver Jackson died."

"I thought it was just because Jackson confessed to the murders. Besides he was being watched by his friends not Sgt. Benton," said a person from the Ranchers table.

"All that is true but a misunderstanding is not much of a motive for murder and he had no motive to kill Paul White. Now what about Jake Pitts?"

Jake had been looking at the floor this whole time. With the mention of his name he looked up. His interest was now peaked.

"Jake's Dad had just been given the family business. When Dad died he would get it all. Now some of you may know that Jake has no interest in running the railroad. But, unlike his Dad, Jake loves television. He likes that his family owns stock in the network. Paul White and Oliver Jackson were actually both biding to buy the network stock from his Dad. Jake probably didn't like that. But why kill his Grandfather? If

Henderson Pitts Sr. was murdered I don't think it could have been Jake. Pitts Sr. didn't believe that Jackson was the killer but he didn't know who it was. Jake and his Grandfather were friends. He had a Father who didn't understand him and an Uncle who wasn't very close. His only friend in the family was Henderson Pitts Sr. I don't think it was Jake Pitts."

"Now we come to Henderson Pitts the second. He is the oldest and should have been the one to inherit the family business. But he was passed over. He has a bad temper but family means a lot to him. So he went along just to keep peace in the family. Also, he had nothing against Paul White or Oliver Jackson. I don't suspect him."

"Two more that we have looked into are Len White and Brandon Parks."

Hearing his name mentioned Parks stands straight up. He glares at me and it boors to the center of my being.

"YOU SAID I WASN'T A SUSPECT!" shouts Parks.

"I said not at that moment. But what you said after that got me to thinking. You found out that Pitts was going to sell the stock cheap to either Jackson or White. That would lower the value of the network and you would have to lay off some workers. Most of your anger was directed at Pitts but if White and Jackson were dead there were no other bidders. White was killed first but Jackson was killed after Pitts. Why kill Jackson if another member of the Pitts family would get the stock. After all they all wanted to keep the stock. But if Oliver Jackson knew who the killer was then he had to die. Now why would you kill Henderson Pitts Sr.? You had no reason to kill him. He didn't know who the killer was. He only knew that it wasn't Jackson. You aren't the killer. Besides if you were that would be harder for the network to rebound from then low stock prices. Who wants to watch TV shows that are being shown by a network of killers."

"That leaves only Len White." Said Sgt. Benton from the corner of the car.

White stands up.

"I didn't do it."

"Well let's examine the evidence now. Garfield Pitts was coming on to your friend Jean. You stood up for her by knocking Pitts down. He tried to get back at you by starting a rumor that could ruin your marriage and your career. It didn't but it almost ruined Jean's. Suddenly into your life comes your distant cousin Paul. It isn't a close family tie but he is family and you have lunch with him from time to time. While his plan for revenge didn't work but it did almost get Jean's program canceled till you threaten to quit your show if that happened. So Jean kept her job. He show was doing well but now it was a low rated program. Garfield Pitts is still making advances to Jean he tells her that he plans to sell all his stock for almost nothing and that would get all the mid to lower rated programs canceled. Jean is near the breaking point. She tells you what she knows. During your many lunches with your cousin he tells you he wants to increase his shares in the network. You tell him that you know Pitts wants to sell for almost nothing.

You hope this will finally get Pitts out of yours and Jeans lives.

However, when Pitts hears from Paul he looks into it and finds that he is your cousin. Pitts increases the amount he wants. This way he gets back at you and makes a profit. None of this sits well with Oliver Jackson. He was the only one interested till Paul White came along. He doesn't have as much money as your cousin and he sees he chance slipping away. He goes to your cousin and tries to convince him to not buy. The argument gets heated and Jackson accidentally kills your cousin. You find out and think the argument was with Pitts and that he killed him. Once on the train you kill Pitts in revenge and after seeing he didn't like Peter you allow him to take the fall. But Jackson is feeling guilty. He goes to confess to the Paul White murder and you know that will point the finger at you for the killing of Garfield Pitts. You kill Oliver Jackson and make it look like he killed them both. But you didn't know that we had another note that he wrote the night before. When compared to the suicide confession note the handwriting didn't match so we knew the killer was still on the loose."

"This is all just fiction. How do I know you have that note?"

I pull it out of my pocket and show it to him. He tries to grab it but I pull back.

"Sorry but this is evidence."

"But I didn't kill anybody. What reason do I have to kill Henderson Pitts Sr.?"

"I don't know. Maybe through word of mouth you know we are still looking for the killer. So you just pick someone at random and kill them."

"If that were true why would I make it look like a heart attack?"

"That, along with some other information that I have uncovered tells me that you are…innocent."

With that good news Len White slumps back in his chair. He is relieved that at the end of this trip he won't be going to jail.

Henderson Pitts Jr. stands and turns toward me. He points his finger and waves it at me.

"Now wait a minute. You've just about cleared everyone you suspected. You said you knew who the killer was. Now who is it?"

I began to pace around the car. Then I turned and looked up at Pitts Jr.

"Well Mr. Pitts there is one person here who knew the deceased better then they said they did."

I went back to the table and Mike handed me the wire that I had shared with them.

"I have here a wire that I got last night. It's from my editor whom I asked to look into the background of the people on this train."

There was quite a ruckus raised with that information.

"Now don't worry. I found out more information on some of you then I cared to know. But it was a military record that caught my attention."

Some people seemed to squirm with that news.

"This person was in the Army during the Korean War. He was not a remarkable solider but he was in the same outfit with Oliver Jackson. Weren't you…"

I dramatically turned and faced him. "…Sgt. Benton."

"I might have been," said a stunned Benton.

"That doesn't mean I knew him."

"You may not have been friends but you knew him. You see there was a long and hard battle that was fought over a piece of ground. It was becoming a blood bath and our side was losing. Word came late to retreat. Jackson got the word in time and obeyed his order. No one would have blamed him if he didn't go back in but Jackson's buddies were still in there. He went back but only found one. The one person that he was able to pull out in one piece was Frank Benton and that is why Jackson was given his medal for bravery."

"So he saved my life that doesn't prove anything."

"You're right if that was the only thing it wouldn't be enough proof. But we also have Oliver Jackson's phone records. A few days before the train left he called you. Then Paul White was killed the next day. He called you again the morning this train left. Then Garfield Pitts was dead. Knowing you were now a policeman he asked you to influence Paul

White to stop buying the stock that Pitts had for sale. Now maybe there was an argument and you killed him or maybe you thought it was a good way to repay your debt to Jackson for saving your life. You tell Jackson he's worried but believes you when you tell him it was an accident. But then you meet with Garfield Pitts and he refuses to sell to Jackson. Again it seems like your temper or your warped sense of duty took over and you shot Pitts. "

"You're grasping at straws."

"Maybe but if you recall I noticed that there were pieces of a glass bottle missing from around the outline of Pitts body in the Baggage car."

"What's that got to do with it?" asked someone from the back of the car.

"What most people don't know is that a bottle on the end of a gun can muzzle a shot. But a military man or a police man would know. You said earlier when you arrested Peter that you came in because you heard a shot. But you didn't hear a shot because you fired it yourself and it was silenced. Later when I found the pieces you knocked me out and took them because they would point out that you couldn't have heard the shot and make you look like a liar. This killing was clear cut premeditated murder. You had planned to kill Pitts if you didn't like his answer."

"This is just all show Adams because I fingered your pal Tork. You have nothing and are grasping at straws. If Jackson saved my life and I wanted to pay him back why would I kill him?"

"That's the easiest one to figure out. You probably told him you killed White and he believed it was an accident. But now Pitts was dead. Jackson put two and two together and was feeling guilty that he ever asked for your help. He told you that he was going to confess to us. Now you see the man who saved your life years earlier may be able to end your life. The only way to stop further investigation is to kill Jackson. This time you strangle him and hang him from a rope to make it look like suicide. You write a note and put it in his pocket to finger him as the killer. That would have ended it but you didn't know he slipped me a note and we all saw that the handwriting didn't match. For those of you who don't know the note was for me to meet him in the Dining car to tell me something. It was when I was leaving to meet with him that Jean Feldon found his body."

"OK! Let's say all this is true. Why would I kill Henderson Pitts Sr.? He didn't know who the killer was."

"He didn't know for certain but he had been looking into it. When he said you must have known some brave and smart men from your line of work and other activities and called you a Private that was his way of letting you know he knew of your military record."

"This is crazy. I won't listen to any more."

Benton starts to leave but Brandon Parks and Len White stood up and blocked his way.

"We stayed to hear his accusations on us," said Parks.

"I think you should sit down pardner," said White.

Feeling slightly intimidated Benton took his seat.

"So now I killed Pitts Sr. because he suspected I was the killer. Adams it was a heart attack. He didn't get to his medicine in time. He almost didn't make it when you and I visited him earlier."

"That may be true and since there is no Doctor on the train we normally would have to wait till we got to Clarksville to have an autopsy done. But we can test something."

"What?"

"His medicine." I took a bottle of medicine out of my pocket and held it in my hand for all to see.

"How will that prove anything?"

"We all just assumed that he didn't get to his medicine in time. What if he did? But the inside of the capsules were replaced with something else. Something like…well I don't know…maybe candy. Yes if you crush hard candy on the inside of these capsules they would look like the same medicine. How about if we test it?"

I took a napkin from the table and opened one of the capsules on to it.

"Maybe we should all take a small taste."

I wet my fingertip and start to touch part of the insides of the now empty capsule. That is the moment when Benton pulls out his gun and blocks the door.

"Alright! So I did do it. I was hoping that if I helped Jackson he could get me a better paying job but he had such high morals. You're right he was going to turn me in and I thought Pitts Sr. knew too. I couldn't go to jail. Now I'm going to cut this car loose. For you this really will be your last train to Clarksville."

Suddenly Peter, Mike, Davy and Micky tried to rush him. Benton fired. Peter went down. Benton went out the door.

"Peter are you ok?" asked Mike.

Peter was holding his leg and grimaced in pain but he still answered.

"I'll be ok but someone has to stop him."

With that assurance the four of us left the car. He wasn't outside the immediate door so we ran through the next car. He wasn't in there for just as we got to the end we saw his foot go off the top rung of the ladder that led to the top of the car. Micky and I climbed up after him.

The wind rushed by as the train sped on to its destination.

"Benton! You'll never get away with this," said Micky.

For some reason Benton turned around and rush straight toward us. We both tried to grab him but it was hard to keep our balance on top of the car. He easily pushes us both aside. I grabbed hold of the top of the car and held on for dear life. Micky was pushed to the other side and I could only hope he did the same thing. I could see Benton start down the ladder again but then Davy and Mike tried to grab him. Mike was kicked in the face and fell to the ground. He stepped on Davy's hand and he lost his grip and also fell off the ladder to the platform. Benton then decided to jump to the next car top. I was still holding on to the side. I was trying to pull myself up but not having much luck. Actually if it wasn't for the danger involved it was a pretty good view of everything. I saw Mike and Davy get themselves together. They then went up the ladder on the car Benton was now on. Mike was off first and took off running towards Benton. Davy was up next and not far behind. For a big man Benton was pretty fast.

"Give me your hand." Said a voice from above.

I looked up and was thankful to see that Micky had survived his near death experience. I reached up as far and as fast as I could with my left hand. Mick grabbed it and pulled me up. As we looked ahead to the next car we saw that Benton had stopped running and was facing Mike and Davy. He had once again pulled out his gun and was pointing it right at Mike and Davy who had stopped dead in their tracks.

"Should we jump to the car to help them?" I asked.

"No way man. What good would that do? He already has the gun pulled. If we get on that car it will just spook him. He may kill Mike or Davy."

With the noise of the train it was hard to hear what was being said. I could make out Davy saying "Give it up mate." But that was it.

Just then I could see the train starting to go around a bend. Beyond that was an over pass. I yelled and Mike turned around. He couldn't hear us but Micky and I pointed ahead of him. When he turned back he and Davy both noticed. I couldn't hear them but they were yelling something to Benton. The overpass got closer and Benton was still waving his gun. As Micky and I ducked, I could see Mike and Davy do the same. Benton just stood there and the bottom of the overpass hit the top of his head. It got dark as we went into the tunnel. As we came out the four of us stood up and looked toward Benton. He was not there. I looked behind us to see if there was any sign of him on the ground. All I saw was the tracks. There was no sign of Benton.

Micky and I made our way down the ladder of our car. Mike and Davy went to the one where Benton was standing in front of and went down. We all met back in the Dining car. Mike and Davy said they didn't find Benton. We could only believe that he died when he hit that overpass. The Waiter finally asked if anyone wanted anything to eat. None of the passengers were very hungry.

I noticed that Samantha and Jean were taking care of Peter. The bullet only scratched his right leg. This was one time I wasn't jealous that another guy had Samantha's attention.

Chapter 32

Later that afternoon the train pulled into the station in Clarksville, Indiana. I had finished my article about this trip hours ago and wired it to my editor. He had kept quiet on it as long as he could and he must have sent it to every news organization in the country. The whole platform was filled with people who wanted to see us. Half of them were reporters trying to get any information they could about our little adventure.

I heard shouts of names coming from the mass of people as we got off the train. I don't know why Mike, Micky, Davy and Peter tried to ignore them but when I heard them call my name I thought it would be better if I kept any information I had for the Fab Tab. Brandon Parks was in his element. He took center stage almost as soon as he got off the train.

"People! People!" he said trying to quiet the crowd. "I can't hear all of your questions if you ask them at the same time. We have all had a very long and tiring trip. I'll try to set up a press conference later. For now we would all like to get to our hotel rooms and finally get some rest."

Micky and I slipped away and soon Jean Feldon and Len White caught up to us.

"That was some trip wasn't it fellas," said Len.

"It was a rough one," said Micky.

"I hope there are no hard feelings in what we revealed Mr. White," I said.

"None at all. Someone had to be the detective."

"Benton sure wasn't going to reveal the killer," said Jean.

"You five did a fine job," said Len.

"One of you should probably write a book about this," said Jean.

"Everyone with half a brain thinks he can write a book," said Micky. "Just look at the guy who wrote this one."

After Jean and Len left I saw Jake Pitts and his Uncle. As Micky and I approached them Jake saw us coming and held up his hand. We stopped.

"There's no hard feelings guys. As a matter of fact I want to thank you for your help. But my Uncle and I are exhausted and want to get some rest before the convention starts tonight. We'll have to help MC it since that is what Dad was going to do."

"I understand that," I said "But there is something you should know. My editor had a hard time convincing your attorney but he did get some information about the will when he told him about the circumstances on the train. It seems that your Dad had a change of heart about the stock he owned in the Television network. He wanted you to have the stock if he died. You're the capable person he kept referring to when he was asked what he was going to with the stock shares."

I turned to his Uncle.

"He also left the railroad business to you."

With that Henderson Pitts the second smiled.

"I always knew he had a soft spot in his heart for family. Thanks for telling us. Let's go Jake. If you need any advice on how to handle the stock just let me know."

"Thanks Unc."

As Jake and his Uncle went their own way and Samantha came up from behind.

"Hi guys!"

"Hey Sam," said Micky.

"That's one trip I am glad is over."

"Me too," I said. "Say Samantha, would you like to have dinner with me tonight?"

"I'd love to Josh but I already made plans for dinner."

Just then Mike and Davy approached us.

"Well Davy," I said. "I hope you have fun on your dinner date tonight."

"What dinner date? I don't have plans for tonight."

"Josh," said Samantha. "I never said it was with Davy."

Just then Peter hobbled up to us.

"I look forward to tonight Peter."

"Me too Sam."

"Let me help you to your hotel."

She grabbed his arm and off they went.

The four of us stood there and watched them walk away in disbelief. Then I turned to Davy. I placed my hand on his shoulder.

"Come Mr. Jones. Let us drown our sorrows in Coca-Cola. My treat."

The four of us then walked to the restaurant that was next to the train station. With that we closed the case on the last train to murder.

The Project: Hero saga continues in Project: Hero Atlantis Under Attack. On sale now from Dinky Publishing.

Also from Dinky Publishing is the book that started it all. A great Christmas story for the kids. Dinky the Elf!

The Old Grey Mare

By Christopher Brockow © 2013

Setting: The Monkees Pad

It's a nice, sunny and warm Sunday afternoon. Davy Jones is walking on the beach and is talking to a pretty blonde hair girl, whom he had just met a few moments before this story started.

The two walk to Davy's beach house where Micky, Mike and Peter were about to practice a set of songs. Davy walked in through the back screen door, right behind Micky and his drums. He introduced his new friend to the boys;

DAVY: Hi guys, I want you to meet Valleri.

As Davy pointed to each one, he remarked :

DAVY: Valleri, this is Mike.

Mike with his guitar in hand, picked up Valleri's hand.

MIKE: Nice to meet you.

DAVY: This is Micky.

Micky sitting behind his drums lifted up his hand with a drum stick.

MICKY: Hello.

Davy took her to the last member.

DAVY: and this is Peter.

Peter with his bass in his left hand uses his right hand and shakes Valleri's hand.

PETER: Hi.

DAVY: Valleri works for Colgems record label.

Micky getting very excited, got up from his chair, tripping over his high hat symbols, speaks to her.

MICKY: You work for Colgems? Could you get us an audition?

Valleri: Sorry boys, I'm not going to be your Stepping Stone.

Mike turns his head with a disgust look on his face, and makes a statement to everyone.

MIKE: I knew this wasn't going to be a Pleasant Valley Sunday.

Peter very innocently makes a sincere suggestion.

PETER: We can always call my *Auntie Grizelda.*

Mike, Davy and Micky altogether: No Peter.

VALLERI: Well boys, it was nice meeting you. Hopefully you will get that record deal you want so badly.
She turns towards Davy, gives him a kiss on the cheek.

VALLERI: Give me a call sometime.

DAVY: I sure will.

Valleri walks out the back sliding door. At the same time a young man whom The Monkees know very well comes visiting. It is Jonathan Fisher with his horse Jeremy.

JONATHAN: Hi guys, Jeremy and I came to see you.

The Monkees Theme

DAVY: (looking at Jonathan) How are you and Jeremy doing?

Jonathan walks in with Jeremy behind him.

MIKE: I don't think Jeremy should come in. Mr. Babbitt would somehow find out.

MICKY: Come on Mike. How is he going to know?

MIKE: Somehow he always does.

(sound of pounding on the front door)

BABBITT: Okay you guys!!!!! I know you have a horse in there! I can smell him!!!!!!

MIKE: You see. What did I tell you?

MICKY: I can always do my werewolf imitation again.

MIKE: No that wouldn't be good.

Mr. Babbitt is still knocking and yelling at the front door.

BABBITT: Are you going to let me in or what?

MIKE: Davy, Peter, help Jonathon back Jeremy out the back

162

there.

As Davy, Peter and Jonathan get the horse outside, Micky picks up a can of Lysol and sprays the whole living area. Mike opens up the door to let Mr. Babbitt in.

As Mr. Babbitt walks in, he starts yelling at the boys.

BABBITT: I told you before...No Pets Allowed, Especially Horses!!!!!!

MIKE: The horse isn't ours. He belongs to our friend Jonathan.

MICKY: That's right Mr. Babbitt. And they are outside. They just came over to visit with us.

BABBITT: Okay, as long as they just visit. But they better not stay here or I will raise your rent!!

After he said his peace, Mr. Babbitt walked out slamming the front him behind him.

MICKY: (sighs) That was close.

Davy, Peter and Jonathan come back inside while Jeremy is outside looking in.

DAVY: (looking at Jonathan) How are you and Jeremy doing?

JONATHAN: I'm fine but it's Jeremy that I'm concerned about.

MICKY: What's wrong?

We will find out what's wrong after this commercial break.

Peter, Micky, Mike and Davy get up on a sunny morning. They go downstairs to eat breakfast. Half asleep Peter grabs a box of Rice Krispies from the cabinet.

Micky gets everyone bowls while Davy gets the spoons.

Mike gets Bordon milk from the refrigerator.

When the boys pour the milk over their cereal, they wake up to that 'Snap, Crackle, Pop sound'.

After eating their cereal, The Monkees put their bowls in the sink, put away the milk and went out to the beach.

And now back to our program

MICKY: What's wrong?

JONATHAN: Jeremy is older and has bad arthritis.

MICKY: Have you tried calling Dr. Mann?

PETER: He could help. He's a veterinarian you know.

MIKE: No. He married. Mrs. Purdy and now they own their own ranch in the mountains.

DAVY: What does your father say about Jeremy?

JONATHAN: Dad did call a veterinarian, but the only thing to do is give him pills.

PETER: I bet they're 'Horse Pills'.

JONATHAN: They only help temporally, but he is not going to get better. Dad can't afford the pills and the Doctor calls. He said we either have to put him down or give him to someone who understands horses.

DAVY: And is that why you came to us?

JONATHAN: Yes. You helped us out the last time. I was hoping you could do it again.

MICKY: But 'that was then and this is now'. Do you want us to come and help out on the farm again?

PETER: We could milk the chickens and get eggs from the cows.

MIKE: Peter, that is milk the cows and get eggs from the chickens. Besides Farmer Fisher did not appreciate our help the last time.

JONATHAN: He did say I could see you guys and see if you could help Jeremy.

DAVY: Let me take a look at him, I know something about horses.

PETER: Davy used to be a jockey. He has a lot of 'Horse Sense'.

Davy walks outside and looks over Jeremy. He takes each leg, one at a time, rubs them, stretches them and checks each hoof to see if the horse shoes are on properly.

After that, Davy gets in the saddle and walks him around the beach.
All The Kings Horses Romp

Setting: Beach outside the Monkees pad.

Davy brings Jeremy back to Jonathan and confirms what was stated earlier.

DAVY: You're right, he does have arthritis, but he can be a pet. Just walk him, nothing more strenuous than that.

JONATHAN: But dad won't let us keep him. He's become too expensive.

Mike, Peter and Micky are standing there thinking what to do. Mike comes up with a suggestion.

MIKE: Maybe he can work somewhere, where he can give kiddie rides.

PETER: Let's try Disneyland.

MICKY: Disneyland won't let us in unless we cut our hair.

DAVY: We should wait 40 years. By then we won't have any hair.

MICKY: By then Disney will be a big corporation and it will be called 'Disney World'.

MIKE: Okay, let's stop with the 'Mickey Mouse' jokes.

PETER: Who writes this stuff?

DAVY: I'll call Valleri and see if she knows where old horses will be cared for.
Davy, Micky, Mike and Peter walk inside while Jonathan stands outside petting Jeremy on his side.

JONATHAN: (talking to Jeremy) Don't worry Jeremy, Davy and his friends will find a good home for you. You will be with someone who can take good care of you and who will love you.

Inside Davy picks up the phone and calls Valleri. (Picture a screen split in two. Davy on one side and Valleri on the other talking on the phone.)

VALLERI: (on the phone) Hello?

DAVY: (on the phone) Hi Valleri, it's Davy.

VALLERI: Hi! What's up?

DAVY: We have a small problem here, it concerns an old horse.

VALLERI: A horse?

DAVY: It is a long story. Do you know of anyone who takes care of older horses with arthritis?

VALLERI: As a matter of fact I do. Her name is Mary and she runs a petting zoo. Mary Mary's Petting Zoo and she is looking for an old horse to give rides to children.

DAVY: That sounds terrific. Can you tell us where she's at?

VALLERI: Better than that, how about I come over and take you to her?

DAVY: Great, we will be waiting for you.

Davy hangs up the phone and tells the others what is going on.

MIKE: *A petting zoo to give little kids horse rides? Isn't that what I suggested earlier?*

MICKY: *Yes you did.*

PETER: *That was a great idea Mike.*

MIKE: *Thanks Peter, Now all we need is a horse trailer.*

Jonathan steps inside to tell the guys.

JONATHAN: *We have one back at the farm.*

Mike, Micky and Jonathan get into the Monkeemobile and head over to Jonathan's farm to pick up the trailer from Farmer Fisher. Once they get to the farm, they hitch the trailer to the end of the car.

Setting: Farm

FARMER FISHER: *I am so glad Jonathan came to you. I didn't want to put that old horse down.*

MIKE: *Don't worry, he's going to get the care that he needs.*

MICKY: *We hope.*

As they drive away from the farm and back to their house, Valleri shows up ready to show everyone where the petting zoo is located.

Setting: Outside the Monkees pad.

Davy leads Jeremy into the trailer, everyone piles into the Monkeemobile and they drive to Mary Mary's Petting Zoo.

We will be right back after this commercial break

Announcer, "After the Monkees work, play and sing, how do they quench a thirst?"
Enter Micky, "Well I grab a Dr. Pepper from the 'fridge'."
Enter Peter, "Micky, are you sick? Do you need a doctor?"
Enter Mike, "No, Peter. He's talking about that original taste you can only find in a can of Dr. Pepper Soda Pop."
Enter Davy, "I drink it because I just like it."
Announcer, "There you have it. Dr. Pepper, original taste that you would just like."

And now back to our program

Setting: Petting Zoo.

When they pull up, they notice the zoo is small but spread out over 15 acres of land. One part has chickens, another goats, there are ducks in a small pond, lambs and mules.

Mary is a well built cowgirl. She is slender, 5'5, long brown hair and she is wearing jeans, short sleeve flannel and a cowboy hat.

MARY: *Welcome to Mary Mary's Petting Zoo. You must be the Monkees and this must be Jeremy.*

DAVY: *Yes we are. And this is Jonathan. I sure hope you can help us out.*

MARY: *I'm sure I can. I need an older horse to give rides to children. Let's see if he will work out.*

JONATHAN: *Don't worry Jeremy, we'll be with you every step*

169

of the way.

Take A Giant Step Romp

As the song is playing, Mary groomed Jeremy, stretched out the leg, cleaned the hoofs and put the saddle back on him. Then she walked him around by the lead. After that she got on his back and walked him in a circle.

She is satisfied by his condition and gave a small boy a trial ride. The young boy likes being on a horse and Mary is very happy about her new pet.

DAVY: I think Jeremy will be very happy here.

PETER: I'm so glad you thought of this Davy.

MICKY: I thought it was Mike who thought of it.

MIKE: You're right, but it was *Valleri who knew Mary.*

DAVY: Thanks Valleri for all your help.

VALLERI: My pleasure.

PETER: All's well that ends well.

MICKY: Until next week.
Everyone gets into the Monkeemobile and they drive back home.

The Monkees are sitting in their director chairs at the sound studio. The announcer gets their attention,

ANNOUNCER: Boys, we are a minute short.

MIKE: Again?

MICKY: You have to time these better.

ANNOUNCER: Tell us about not playing your own instruments.

MIKE: You're right, we don't.

ANNOUNCER: What do you mean?

MIKE: I play a bass and Peter plays a guitar.

PETER: So I'm playing Mike's bass and he's playing my guitar.

MICKY: I play the tambourine and maracas, and Davy bangs on drums.

DAVY: So I am playing Micky's drums and he plays my tambourine and maracas.

ANNOUNCER: Well thanks for clearing that up.

DAVY: Goodbye until next time.

End Credits

**For Pete's Sake
Closing Song**

Get this book to see how Amazing
Fantasy #15 influenced people from
1962 to today.

STORIES OF ONE AMAZING BOOK
THAT CHANGED EVERYTHING
Foreword by Fred Hartley

A Quiet Drive in the Country

By Rick L. Phillips © 2013

It's early 1967 and actor/singer Davy Jones is stuck on the side of the road of a Southern California Highway. The hood of the car's engine is propped up and steam is coming from the engine. Davy is leaning against his car with a sour look on his face.

"This is some way to spend my day off. We finally get a break in our schedule from shooting the show and I take a drive to get away for a while. But I spend half the day with a broke down car." He thinks to himself.

Suddenly a green tow truck with a sign on the side that says Johnson Brothers Service Station slows down and then pulls up in front of his car. A man from the driver's side gets out. He has a beard and is wearing a baseball cap with the Dodgers insignia on the front. He is also wearing a gray tee shirt with blue jeans and brown work boots.

As he walks toward the car he looks at it with a curious look. Then he looks at Davy. Suddenly his face lights up a little bit more. Davy was happy to see the truck but not sure about this man.

"Don't I know you?" Asked the man.

"You may have seen my TV show, The Monkees."

"That must be it. I did see it a couple of times. So what happened here?"

"I don't know. I was just driving along and steam started coming from the engine."

The man looks under the hood.

"I'll tell you what, now I need to get it back to the station to make sure, but it looks like your fan belt broke," said the man. "Don't worry about the cost. I'll give you a good price. Look I can go back and get a fan belt and bring it back."

"How long will it take before you get back?"

"Depending on traffic it can take 20 to 30 minutes for me to get to the station and another 20 or 30 to get back. So you could be here for about an hour. I can send someone back with a car to pick you up."

"It's pretty hot out today. How about if I save us some time and ride back with you in the cab of the truck?"

"Well I don't know. Dale doesn't like anyone else in the cab of the truck but me."

"He probably won't mind on a hot day like this. Maybe I can just sit in my car while you tow it back."

Seeing that Davy is set on going with him he agrees to him riding in the truck. After the man hooked up the car they both got in the truck and left for the service station. As they pulled away and drove down the road the man got on and radioed in to the station.

"Dale, this is Bob calling in."

"When you coming in?" Asked the voice from radio.

"I'm coming in now with a car I saw on the side of the road. The owner is coming in with me."

"Why's the owner with you? You know our insurance only covers you or me in the truck." He said sounding a little angry.

"Come on Dale. It's really hot out today. I couldn't leave him standing out there that long waiting for me to come back."

"Ok, but be careful."

About twenty five minutes later they pulled into the service station's parking lot. As Davy climbed out of the truck he saw a tall, lean man in t-shirt and overalls walking towards him. He had some stubble on his face that looked like he hadn't shaved in a couple of days. He was giving Davy a curious look as he tried to place him.

"You look kind of familiar little fella." Said Dale.

By this time Bob had gotten out of the truck and was about to introduce Davy to his brother but before he could a girl about 18 years old and wearing cut off jeans as short pants comes up and introduces him in her own way.

"Dale don't you know who this is? It's Davy Jones of the Monkees."

"Davy this is my brother Dale and our little sister Sandy." Said Bob.

"Nice to meet you. We don't get too many celebrities out this way." Dale says as he shakes Davy's hand.

Davy puts out his hand to shake Sandy's but Sandy pulls him closer and gives him a big hug around his neck and then gives him a big kiss.

"You certainly are friendly out here," says Davy as he nervously pulls away.

"I just love the Monkees. My favorite song is "A Little Bit Me, A Little Bit You," Sandy tells Davy as she looks at him with love in her eyes.

"It sure is," says Bob as he and Dale look over the car. "She played that song so much Dale almost threw the record away cause he was so tired of hearing it."

While Sandy talks to Davy about the Monkees, Dale and Bob have a quiet discussion by his car as they speak in whispers.

"We can make some money off of this car but we can make even more money off of him."

"What do you mean?" Asked Bob.

"Just go along with me."

Dale turns around and walks toward the entertainer.

"Well you do have a busted fan belt but you also seem to have an oil leak."

"I thought so. I saw some oil spots on the road as we drove back. Can I watch you work under the bonnet?"

"Under the what?" Asked Bob.

"Under the hood as you say in America."

"Well we can't work on it now because we don't have the parts for this car. Bob and I have to go into town and get a transmission for another car we're working on. I'll see if I can get the parts there. Why don't you wait here with Sandy till we get back?"

Davy turns to Sandy to see if that is alright with her but before he can say anything everything goes black. When he wakes up he is in the back of the station and tied and gagged. Sandy is sitting next to him reading an issue of Tiger Beat that has a picture of Peter Tork on the cover.

"Peter is cute but they should have you on the cover every month," she says as she sees Davy has woken up.

Davy tires to talk but she can't understand him with the gag on. She takes it off of his mouth.

"What is going on here?"

"Well Dale and Bob steal auto parts for a living."

"What's that got to do with hitting me and tying me up?"

"Bob and Dale started this station years ago. It did ok for awhile but business slowed down. So Bob started finding abandoned cars on the road. They brought the cars back stripped them down and sold the parts. This time was different. You were still with the car and insisted on coming back with him. After Dale hit you Bob and I got sore at Dale. But you don't stay mad at Dale too long. He has a violent temper. He was getting real mad at us. He thought he could not only sell your car for parts but that he could hold you for ransom. He said the TV stations and record companies would probably pay a million dollars to get you back."

"So you and Bob are helping him."

"We don't really want to. We just don't want to make him mad. Dale would never mean to hurt or kill anyone but he gets so mad that it could happen."

Suddenly there is the sound of a car outside. Sandy looks out the window then turns back toward Davy.

"It's the guys. They're back earlier then I thought they would be."

She goes toward Davy and picks up the gag.

"You're not going to put that back on are you?"

"I'd rather not but Dale won't like it if he sees I took it off." She replies.

After she gags him again she picks up the magazine and sits back down. Just then the door flies open and in steps Dale.

"This is the most money we ever made." He practically shouts as he waves a wad of bills as he comes in.

"Who paid that much money for only one part?" Asked Sandy.

"Not one part the whole car." Replies Bob.

"All we need to do is haul the car to him. When we come back we'll send the ransom notice to the TV station about their star here."

With that the three of them go outside. Davy quickly looks around. He sees a wooden chair nearby. He crawls over to it. He leans on the chair and slowly stands up. His feet and hands are still tied. He looks around the room to see if there is anything that will help free himself.

The sharpest thing in the room is the edge of a table. No broken glass anywhere in the room. He thinks about rubbing the ropes that bind him on it but knows it will take longer than the time he has till they return. Just then Sandy comes back in.

"Ya won't find anything like broken glass in here." She says seeing that he is up and looking around. "I sweep things like that up as soon as it breaks."

She goes over and removes the gag on Davy.

"They've just left so we can talk again."

"You could also untie me since it's just you and me."

"I'd like to but it would take too long to tie you back when they got back."

"Sandy, you seem like a nice girl. I'll tell the police you were forced into this and maybe they will go easy on you. I'll be a character witness for you. Just untie me."

"I can't Dale would kill me."

"He can't if he's in prison."

She looks into his eyes and starts to smile.

"I can't believe that I have dreamt of meeting you and now that I have I've kidnapped you."

"You're not the one who kidnapped me."

"Well I've been helping but not anymore."

She starts to turn Davy around to untie him but stops.

"What are you doing?" Davy asked.

"I may never get this chance again." She replies. Then she plants a deep, long kiss on Davy's lips.

From the look on Davy's face it is clear that he enjoyed the kiss.

"Well we can take a few minutes longer if you want." He says with a slight laugh.

She gives him another kiss but then Davy moves his head back after a few seconds.

"Ok! Really we can finish that later. Right now we have a crime to stop."

She knows he's right and reluctantly turns him around and unties the ropes.

Davy rubs his wrist trying to get circulation back into his arms. He looks at Sandy admiring her as she takes this stand against her brothers.

"Thanks! Now where is your fastest car so I can beat them into town?"

"They took the only running car we have. The rest have been all stripped down for parts."

"Is there anything else that can get me there faster than walking?"

"Just Snyper."

"Who's Snyper?"

"That's my horse. I raised him from a colt."

"I'm great with horses. Can I see him?"

Sandy takes Davy out back. The yard has car parts all over the ground. Beyond there is a pasture with a beautiful wooded hillside.

"I don't see a horse."

"You will in a minute. SNYPER!!!" Yells Sandy.

In a few seconds out of the woods on the hill comes running a beautiful horse. She stops her full gallop right in front of Sandy. As Sandy pets her and talks to her it is clear that there is a special bond between Sandy and Snyper.

"Now Snyper this here is Davy. He is a good and kind man and he needs your help. He needs to get to town real fast. So let him ride you and help him get there."

The horse seemed to know what she said and it snapped to attention.

"Davy you can ride him now. He's ready for you."

Davy climbs on the horse and gets ready to ride him bareback into town.

"We'll be back soon."

Snyper rears up on his hind legs. As he does Davy fights off the urge to shout "Hi-ho Silver" and soon points the horse in the direction of the road and off they go. They are making great time and with the speed that Synper travels he knows that this horse would do well on the racetrack. But it isn't fast enough to beat the huge head start that Dale and Bob have.

"If we just follow the roads we'll get there too late. If they get to town and back before me, Sandy will be in trouble." Thinks Davy to himself. "Some people will hate this but I have to take some drastic measures."

The road takes a sharp turn to the right as next to the road is a wooden fence that outlines the side yard of a home. Davy urges Snyper to go faster. As they approach the bend in the road he won't let the horse take the turn. Instead they head straight for the fence and at the last second Snyper jumps it. They keep on this straight line as they run through yards and pastures. Snyper jumps every obstacle in his path with Davy getting shouts from many of the surprised landowners. At one point Davy got a glimpse of the highway and could see Dale and Bob as they drove into town. He just hoped that they didn't see him.

Soon Davy was in town but Dale and Bob got there just a little bit ahead of him. He quietly guides Snyper through the backstreets so he won't be seen. He arrives at the police station. He ties the horse to a telephone pole and goes in to report his own kidnapping and his car being stolen.

He goes up to the Desk Sergeant.

"Hello, I'd like to report a kidnapping."

"Who and when?"

"Mine and it was about an hour ago."

"But you're here."

"I know I just escaped. They also stole my car and are down the street now trying to sell it."

After a few minutes more of his explanation, Davy is escorted down the street by two patrolmen. As they walk outside the officers see Snyper tied to the pole.

"Are you the one we were getting calls about leaping through people's yards on a horse?"

"It was the only way I could get here without my car."

"We can overlook that considering what you've been through."

Davy directs them to where he last saw his car. To his surprise it's still there with Bob and Dale standing next to it. As soon as they see the Police they run down an alley. One Policeman takes off after them while the other runs around the building.

"Halt! Police!" Shouts the one running after them. But they don't stop. Staying at the entrance of the alley where the chase started is Davy. He watches as the two near the end of the ally. They had a head start and because of that they may get away. Just as they are about to turn the corner the other Policeman jumps in front of them with his gun drawn. Knowing they are caught they put their hands up. The Police arrest them and take them back to the station.

As Davy goes back out he starts to untie Synper from the pole.

"What are you doing?" Asked one of the Policemen from behind him.

"Well I have to ride him back."

"No you can't."

"You're right I'll have to take my car. Who will take care of the horse?"

"The Police will have to take care of both. They're now part of our investigation. We've been looking for these car thieves for almost a year. We may be able to train the horse to work with the Police. We can use a good Police horse. He can help us stop all those people jumping fences in the backyards." He said as he gave Davy a smile.

Davy smiled back but then looked concerned.

"Well how will I get home?"

"Before I came out I was told to take you back to the city. They sent someone else out to arrest the girl."

"Make sure they go easy on her please. Without her help I wouldn't have escaped."

A couple of days later Davy was back at the studio to work on the TV show. Micky and Peter were talking about a party that Peter had at his house. Mike said he took his family on a picnic. Then Micky looked at Davy.

"You've been awful quiet. What did you do this weekend?"

"Oh, I just went for a nice quiet drive in the country."

MAMA'S BOYS-THE ADVENTURES OF DAVY AND BRUCE

By Steven Thompson © 2013

What follows is a parody. It is an amusing tale of what might have been and features characters based not just on Davy Jones but also on other real people. As this is a parody, it in no way reflects what these people were or are like in real life. In point of fact, the actions, statements and beliefs of any and all characters herein are not intended to reflect reality in any way whatsoever. This is a protected parody...and it all began on a Monday afternoon in 1972 in a place where many things begin in Hollywood—a casting director's office.

"I'm sorry, Mr. Jones but we won't be able to use you in this new show," he said with a failed attempt not to laugh. "There are no...monkeys... in our script." He had emphasized the word "monkeys," a word Davy had quickly begun to hate as much as he had once loved it.

"Right, then," was Davy's reaction through gritted teeth. "S'very funny, mate. Hilarious, innit?" With that he turned and stepped back out into the waiting room without looking back except when he slammed the door. It was at that point that he accidentally bumped into a neatly dressed Asian man wearing dark glasses who was NOT amused.

"Watch it, man!" he barked gruffly.

Davy took a deep breath and released it. "Sorry, mate. Cheers."

The man he had run into put his hand firmly on Davy's shoulder and said, "Hold on, hold on. I recognize you. You're Davy Jones of the Monkees. What's got you so hopped up?"

"That's just it. I'm Davy Jones! 'Of the Monkees' is not part of my name! Never HAS been! And besides, I'm NOT even a Monkee anymore! The show is over. The band is over! Yet everyone still pigeonholes me as 'Davy Jones of the Monkees!'"

Chuckling, the Asian man removed his shades. "I know what you mean. My show's been off the air now for several years and at every casting office in town, I'm still 'Kato from The Green Hornet.'"

Recognition dawns. "Wait a minute! You're Bruce Lee. I've 'eard about you. What are you doing 'ere?"

"Apparently auditioning for the same show that just turned you down, my friend. A man's gotta eat. I developed a Western with Warner Brothers as a vehicle for myself and then they went and cast a Caucasian in it!"

"A western? You're serious?" Bruce nodded. "Oh, that would be great! I've always been good with horses, you know! But, yeah, with your looks and my accent, who's ever gonna cast us in a western?" He turned toward the glass door he had just slammed and said, "And trust me, you don't want to go in there! It's only Monday and I'm already ready to..."

The casual banter from the two disenfranchised actors was suddenly interrupted with music as a woman who had been sitting in one of the waiting room chairs all along, hidden

187

behind an open newspaper, began to warble, "Monday, Monday. Can't trust that day..." She lowered the paper and was instantly recognized by the duo.

"Holy...Mama Cass? What are YOU doing here?" said Davy.

She was a large woman, about 300 pounds, attired in a bright pink pantsuit adorned with red flowers at the neck. She spoke as she rose from the chair. "See. That's exactly what you guys were just talking about. Now, I haven't been with the Mamas and the Papas for a few years and yet you still see me as 'Mama' Cass. I guess I'll always be a Mama and YOU will always be a Monkee."

"Well, I know one thing," said Lee. " I will NOT always be Kato. I'm going to Hong Kong soon to star in some martial arts movies that will make me a STAR!"

"Uh-uh, honey. Not in the US. Americans just aren't ready for an Oriental movie star."

Bruce looked as though he were about to argue the point but Davy interrupted. "Say, you still haven't told us. What ARE you doing here?"

"Me?" she chuckled with a bright smile. "Why, waiting for you two, of course."

"No, seriously."

"Trust me, boys. I'm being serious when I say, 'Uncle Sam wants you!'"

"What?" Davy spouted. "They're gonna try and draft me again? I've already been through all that mess! I'm not even American!"

"We can work on that. Hey, let's go somewhere where we can talk privately and I'll explain, okay? Come on. I'm buyin'."

"But what about my audition?"

"Oh, skip it, Bruce. Davy's right. This show'll never get off the ground. Another thing Middle America will never accept is two girls and a guy living together on television!"

A short trip down the street to a quiet restaurant found the trio sitting in a back booth, shielded from prying eyes.

"Here's how it is, fellas. The United States government has been recruiting agents from within the ranks of show business for years. People who are currently 'at leisure,' if you will. I work for a specially created top-secret government organization SO secret it doesn't even have a name.

Davy looked puzzled. "But I don't get it? I thought you were a hippie chick? Free love and getting high. Anti-establishment and all that!"

"Yeah, that hippie thing's been over a while, too," she answered as she shook her head. "You TV people really do lead a sheltered life. The most recent thing I've done was a guest spot on the SCOOBY DOO cartoon series."

"Hey! I was on that as well!"

Bruce frowned and looked down at the table. "Not me. They didn't even ASK me. Darn it. And I love cartoons!"

"Okay, okay. Well, here's the deal. We need you guys for a particular assignment. We'll put you two up in an apartment. Nobody will think twice about two out of work actors hanging out together but in reality you'll be working for us."

Once again, Bruce looked annoyed. "Nothin' doing. I have a wife and kids you know! Why would I leave them to move in with THIS guy? That kind of thing can hurt a guy's reputation!"

"And I'm not single either! This is ridiculous. Forget it. Not interested."

"Fellas, fellas...! It'll just be for two weeks. Here's what it pays. Cass wrote a number on one of the napkins and slid it across the table to where they could see it.

"Linda can get along for a few weeks without me. I'm in."

"Me, too. Who do you want killed?"

"Ha. Ha. Hopefully it won't come to that," she said. "Not like last time."

Davy scrunched his face together and said, almost comically, "Last time??"

"Sorry. I misspoke. Just forget it. Nothing to do with this case. Still top secret. But messy...very messy."

"Right, then, " said Davy as he got up from the table. "I've changed me mind."

"Oh, sit down. I'll protect you," said Bruce calmly.

"You?? You don't really think all that karate jazz you did on TV would do any good in real life, do you? You're knockered!"

Bruce rose and his temper was clearly rising with him. "It. Was. Not. Karate! I do Jeet Kune Do!" With that, Bruce jumped up, emitted an ear-piercing screech and loudly shattered the ornate light fixture over the table with a lightning fast kick. Davy's mouth hung open.

Mama Cass yelled across the floor, "Put it on my bill, Yossarian! Here. Bruce..., Davy. Sit back down and let me tell you WHY we need YOU two and nobody else for this assignment. There you go. Oh, take that look off your face, Bruce, or I'll sit on you.

For just a fraction of a second, a smile crossed Bruce Lee's lips. "Sorry."

Davy was still nervous but sat back down. "Look, I mean, violence is not my bag, you know? It's a bad trip."

Cass used her large hands and arms to casually brush all the remaining bits of the now crackling light fixture from the tablecloth onto the floor. "Have either of you ever heard of Kazbistan?" Blank stares greeted her query. "I'll take that as a 'no.' I'm not surprised. Kazbistan is one of those new mini-oil regimes that seem to pop up all the time lately. Most of them sign various treaties and get swallowed up by the larger oil-producing nations and in a year or two they're forgotten. In this case, it was land given to a Prince by his father. Being in the desert, they looked and, what do you know? They found oil on it! So for right now, at least, Kazbistan is one of the most important nations in the world...even though it's not much bigger than Rhode Island."

"So you're sending us to the Middle East?" asked Bruce.

"Oh, no. The Middle East is coming here! Prince Achmendat is arriving in the US next week to race his prize Arabian stallion in the Million Dollar Hollywood Stakes."

"I've got tickets to that. I've got a thing about horses, you know!"

"That's why we need you, Davy."

"And what about me?"

"Bruce, we need you because we have intelligence that a group of deadly Chinese assassins will try to get to the Prince while he's on US soil and create an international incident. Until Kazbistan gets swallowed up whole by a larger country—and history shows that it will—Uncle Sam needs to be on their good side."

"So," pondered Davy, "What exactly do you want from us?"

"Like I said, we'll set you up in an apartment. You'll be seen around town together over the next week so the two of you spotted at the Stakes next weekend hopefully won't raise any red flags." Once again, she grabbed a napkin and wrote on it. "Here's your new address. Just tell your families that you'll be rehearsing for a new show."

"And who's paying for the cab there?" Davy inquired.

"Oh, didn't I mention? You guys have got wheels. C'mon." With that she rose, placed some large bills on the restaurant table and exited with Bruce and Davy. Outside, they were stunned to see what she meant.

Parked in front of the restaurant was a familiar, sleek red car. "It's the flippin' Monkeemobile! What th...?!"

Bruce ran his hands over the sleekness of its body. "The Brucemobile you mean! This is awesome. My buddy McQueen would kill for this!"

"Ey! I should know the Monkeemobile when I see it! Even if the logo HAS been painted over! How'd it get here anyway? It wasn't parked here when we went in."

"Secrets. They become second nature in this job, boys. Anyway, it's not the original Monkeemobile but a tricked up copy. We want you two to be noticed and figured this would do it. But it's got some surprises, too."

"You mean it's got an ejector seat so I can get rid of Judomaster, here?"

"Judo?? You ignorant Englishman! If you keep that up, I'll show you '"judo'."

"Wow. Listen to your Mama and stop fighting! You have to be a team on this. Got it?" The two stared at each other intently. "I said, 'GOT IT?'" Davy and Bruce nodded.

Bruce held out his hand but Davy just looked at it. "Sorry, gov. Let's build that trust thing slowly, right?"

Over the next week, Davy and Bruce made a point of being seen everywhere together—restaurants, premieres and various Hollywood functions and ceremonies. Every night they were out driving in the familiar car whose name they argued over constantly! Mama made sure that word got out to all the right gossip columnists that the pair were huddling together closely to work on ideas for a top secret film project. In a town like Hollywood, far stranger things have happened in the name of art. No one would be the least bit suspicious of seeing the two unlikely pals together around town.

Behind the scenes, however, they were being given daily briefings on their real mission. Davy was sitting awkwardly across a comfy chair in front of the television watching a rerun of GILLIGAN'S ISLAND when Bruce called out from the next room, "Have you heard anything from our contact yet?"

"I called the number half an hour ago and left a message with someone. They said he was on his way."

"Ding DONG!"

"That must be him, now. You wanna get that?"

"Me? I'm working out in here," called Bruce back from the next room, "trying to keep myself limber. You get it this time!" Davy scowled in Bruce's direction and jumped up from his comfortable sprawl.

"Ding-DONG" went the apartment's doorbell again. Davy padded across the plush lavender carpet and peeked out through the peephole in the door.

"Oh my gosh!" he said as he opened the door to see actor Bob Denver.

"You rang?"

"I was just watchin' you on the telly!"

Bob looked across the room and saw himself splashing into a lagoon in fading color before it cut to a commercial. "Oh, groovy! I'll probably get a buck or two in residuals. That thing runs so often I hardly see any money from it anymore."

At that moment, Bruce came in toweling himself off. "You? You are our contact today?"

"Yup. Lovable ol' me. Cass can be very persuasive and hey, it's good money when the parts aren't coming. Also she scored me tickets to see CSN last month!"

Davy waved the lanky Denver into the room and toward a table. "SKIPPERRR!" echoed his voice from the past.

"Can we turn that off, please?"

"Oh, sorry." Bruce walked over to the television in the corner to click it off.

"Cass said this would be the last briefing—the big one," Davy noted.

"Yup." As he sat at the marble-topped table, Bob pulled several large manila envelopes out of his bag and out of each, some large black and white photographs.

"Today's Saturday. Prince Achmendat is arriving at the airport today at Noon on a private chartered flight from Kazbistan. His prize stallion will be taken immediately to the track to be put on exhibition before Sunday's race."

Davy looked deeply at the racehorse in one of the pictures. Bob noticed this and looked at Davy. "A fine piece of horse flesh, huh?"

"E's gorgeous!" Davy responded. "What's his name?"

"Here's his stats," Bob replied, handing Davy another page. "His name, as you can see there, is Daydream Believer."

At that moment, Davy could have been knocked over with a feather. "You mean the Prince is a Monkees fan?"

"Actually, our intelligence think it's pure coincidence. But it sure gives a great opening for you to be able to connect with the Prince."

"And just how," asked Bruce, "are two ex-TV stars going to get within a hundred feet of this Prince anyway?"

"Oh, that's all arranged, buddy. He's having a celebrity open house this afternoon at 3 at the Hilton. While the horse goes off to the track, the Prince wants to meet Hollywood royalty. Everybody's gonna be there—Raquel Welch, Goldie Hawn, Jill St. John, Natalie Wood, Stefanie Powers—all the big name stars."

"'Ey, wait a minute. Those are all women. Aren't there any men going to be there?"

"Yeah," chimed in Bruce, "and they aren't exactly the biggest names in Hollywood either!"

"There'll be men there—you two. Oh, and maybe Cary Grant if his schedule permits. Remember, the Prince will be schmoozing trying to make international deals as well as good will. The fix is IN at the track to allow his horse to win if only to avoid embarrassment that could lead to an international incident."

"But what about the assassins? That's what you guys needed US for isn't it?"

"That's just it. You two will stick close to the Prince all afternoon to make sure nothing happens. He doesn't know you're working for us. He doesn't know there's been a credible threat. He doesn't know..."

"Blimey, he probably doesn't know who WE are even!"

"Here are your passes to get in. Flash these to security and you're cleared all the way to His Royal Highness's penthouse."

"I was hoping we'd get to see the horse."

"Don't worry about the horse. He's just something you and the Prince have in common so you can keep him talking as needed. And Bruce, you just keep an eye out for suspicious activities otherwise."

"Who are these assassins anyway?"

"We're not sure but we have it on good authority they're sponsored by the Red Chinese."

"One? Two? Fifty?"

"No idea. I can't imagine they could sneak a big group in but you never know, you know? Everything else you need to know is in these packets. Any questions?"

"Other than, 'How did we get into this mess?'... no," muttered Bruce.

"Alrighty then. I'm off. Got an audition at 1 for a new syndicated sitcom with Forrest Tucker. Wish me luck! You guys should be at the hotel before 3." With that, Bob Denver rose and scurried out the door leaving Davy and Bruce staring at each other.

Davy broke the silence with, "I've gotta shave."

At quarter 'til three, our heroes arrived at the giant hotel complex where a crowd of celebrity watchers had gathered. Bruce hopped out of the sleek red customized car and tossed the keys to one of the many young men who gathered around for the valet parking. "No joyrides, Junior!"

"Oh, no, sir, sir!"

Davy, meanwhile had lit up his million dollar smile for the crowd and was already signing autographs. Bruce signed a few on his way to catch up, eyeing everyone in the crowd as they worked their way through it. Both men were wearing dark suits and sunglasses but were nonetheless instantly recognizable.

Inside the door, Bruce wondered aloud how come security wasn't tighter. "Anyone out there could be our assassin!"

"Let's not get paranoid," calmed Davy.

"It's not paranoia when I'm right! If we don't know who he is, then he could be any one of those people out there! Or all of them even!" Davy knew his partner was right. It made him nervous just thinking about it.

Soon enough, they found themselves ushered through upstairs security into the Royal Suite. To Davy, it all felt familiar. The throngs of beautiful people and expensive decorations reminded him of two things—the press junkets thrown for the Monkees in the early days and the plots of a couple of actual episodes!

Surveying the elaborate hotel room, Bruce looked for entrances and exits. Davy looked for the host. Expecting the Middle-Eastern Prince to be dressed in robes and a headdress, he was extremely surprised when he saw that he was wearing regular clothes, chatting away with Annette Funicello with whom Davy had shared a scene in HEAD. Sauntering over, he stood close by until Annette recognized him and introduced him. "Oh, your Majesty, this is my friend David Jones. He's a recording star. Perhaps you're familiar with his group, The Monkees?"

"No, I have not had the pleasure," said the Prince in a thick but pleasingly musical accent as he extended his hand.

As he grasped it, Davy took the opportunity to immediately seize on their common ground. "Your Majesty, I can't wait to see your horse tomorrow."

"Ah, yes! Daydream Believer is my pride."

"I...uh...actually had a hit record called 'Daydream Believer.'"

"No...! You jest?"

"Oh, no! Really! It was one of the Monkees' biggest hits! Written by a man called John Stewart but I sang the song on the recording."

"I must hear this song named after my horse."

"Well, it was actually written a few years ago so it wa..."

"Sing it for me!"

Davy looked around. There were no musicians anywhere. "But...but..."

"Honored guests, Mister David Jones has a song dedicated to my beloved stallion, Daydream Believer." The Prince spoke loudly and began applauding. Everyone else began to applaud as well. Davy eyed Bruce, standing near the balcony watching for anything suspicious. His partner nodded his head.

Sighing deeply, the former Monkee stepped to the center of the room as the crowd opened to allow him a space. Clearing his throat, he said, "I haven't sung this in a while. I hope I remember the words." Then... Davy Jones began to sing.

"Oh, I could hide, 'neath the wings..." As Davy sang, he danced around the crowd, coming face to face with familiar ladies like Margaret O'Brien, Britt Ekland and Nichelle Nichols. So many familiar faces. In fact, they were all familiar. Every single one of the 50 or so celebrities in attendance was a known item. Not one of them could possibly have been the assassin! Davy cut the last refrain and finished to massive applause as he ran to the Prince's side.

"Prince, tell me. How much do you love Daydream Believer?"

"Oh, I enjoyed the song very much, Mister David Jones."

"No, no! The horse, man! Your horse. 'Ow much do you love your horse?"

"That horse is like my equine son. Should anything happen to him..."

"It would cause an international incident, right?"

"Absolutely. My country would be forced to..."

"Bruce! Follow me. We 'aven't got a moment to lose!" Davy ran out the door quickly. Bruce ripped off his jacket and shirt and sprinted topless through the door right behind him.

In the elevator, Bruce asked, "What in the world are we doing? We're supposed to be protecting the Prince."

"Trust me," said Davy. "I can vouch for every single person in that room. Don't you see? It's not the Prince who's in danger. It's Daydream Believer! The horse is who they're after. I'm sure of it!"

When they got outside, Davy looked around at a loss. "Where's our car?"

"Parked in some underground garage somewhere."

"But how are we going to get to..."

At that moment, a Lincoln-Continental pulled up to the curb and as one of the valets approached the driver, Bruce nudged him out of the way. "Park your car, madam?" he said with an ingratiating grin.

"Why, yes, but make sure you don't..."

"Oh, we'll take perfectly good care of it, madam," he said to the matronly driver before turning to Davy and adding, "Get in."

"But..."

"Get in."

As her car roared off down the boulevard with Bruce at the wheel, the woman turned to one of the valets. "Why was that Asian man shirtless?" The valet just shrugged.

It didn't have the coolness factor of the Brucemobile nor did it have the enhanced speed. Still, the black Lincoln reminded Bruce of his days driving Black Beauty. "Hurry!" yelled Davy.

"What? You don't think 50 MPH on a main thoroughfare in the middle of a Saturday afternoon is hurrying? We're lucky we haven't picked up a police escort."

"I'm sorry, man. It's just I'm convinced I'm right. They're going after that horse."

It was only about a 15 minute trip and as the car pulled into the backtrack area by the stables, Davy opened its door and bolted, only to have a very large man step in front of him, stopping him cold. "It's all right, sir," said Bruce. "We're here to inspect the premises to make sure the Prince's horse is safe."

"Where's your shirt?"

"I told you, man! I told you in the car that was stupid idea!" Davy ran past the security man who turned and reached into his jacket. "HA-KAAAA!" yelped Bruce as he kicked the much larger man in the chin until he fell! Then he ran on after Davy. When he caught up with him, he had already found Daydream Believer.

"I swear to you, sir, this horse is as protected as His Majesty himself. The only strange men to come anywhere near him today are you and your shirtless friend there." Davy turned to see Bruce approach. He glowered at him. Bruce shrugged.

"But...Are you sure? Maybe they've just not...Hey! Who's that going in to the stable with a doctor's bag?"

"That is Dr. Draiman. He is the official track doctor who has to sign off on Believer before he will be able to race tomorrow."

"Stop that man!" yelled Davy suddenly and loudly. Bruce started to run toward him when an Oriental man dressed in black jumped out of the tree under which they were standing.

The man surveyed Bruce while Bruce walked around him, sizing him up. "This is no time for a dance, you two!" Davy cautioned. "Oh, I'll do it myself!"

As Bruce and the other man began to yelp and exchange blows, Davy ran at the man he had been told was a doctor and tackled him. The two struggled and a lucky kick sent the older man back over and through a stall window. At that point, Davy mounted the horse bareback and made a clicking noise with his mouth. "Giddyup, boy! Go!" Daydream Believer kicked open the stall door and burst through with Davy, although an experienced jockey, having to hang on tightly. Behind them, the supposed Doctor had pulled a gun and started firing, spooking the horse. He whinnied and reared a bit but Davy held on and encouraged him to keep running by nudging his sides with his feet.

Meanwhile, Bruce was making short work of the would-be assassin. After tossing him around a bit, Bruce flipped the darkly dressed man over his shoulders and ran screaming at the man with the gun.

"Yiiiiiiiiiiiiiiiiiiiii!!!"

The man was momentarily confused and stopped firing just in time for Bruce to spin around and toss his cohort at him.

By that point, the security people had arrived including the one Bruce had earlier gotten around. They held the would-be assassins at bay. Bruce patted the man on the shoulder and smiled.

"No hard feelings."

It was at that point that Prince Achmendat came screeching up in a police car.

"My horse! Where is my beloved horse??!!" Bruce pointed at Davy who came trotting peacefully back up the roadway with the beautiful steed. Bruce smiled and gave him a thumbs up!

Davy dismounted and breathlessly said, "I can explain, Your Highness."

From behind him, he heard a familiar voice. "I explained it to the Prince on the way over."

"Cass?" exclaimed Bruce in surprise.

"Yeah, I was invited to that party, too, fellas. I was just fashionably late. Sorry I missed your song, Davy," she said as she touched his cheek. " I figured out the same thing you must have figured out and so I updated His Majesty and we headed on over here."

"That's great," said Davy. "Whew! That was almost fun!"

"I have to know, though, partner, how did you spot the phony doctor?"

"You forget. I love horses. I've been out here enough to know Dr. Draiman and I know he is NOT Chinese! When I looked at this man walking directly toward the stable even while we were all arguing over the possible dangers, I could see he wasn't the real doctor. 'E probably has the real doc tied up at his office."

"We're already checking on that, fellas," assured Mama Cass.

"This should get us some great publicity in tomorrow's paper, too!"

"Uh-uh, Davy."

"What? Why not?"

"Yeah! Why not? Actors can always use good press!"

"Come on, guys. Be realistic. If word got out that the government was using out of work actors to fight spies and foreign assassins, then where would we be? Naw, your involvement in this will be limited to a curious incident where Davy sang at the celebration and then ran out, while Bruce ripped off his shirt and followed him."

"What?" yelled an outraged Bruce. "That will make us look ridiculous!"

"Cookies. Crumbling. You know how it is. But...Say, you guys DO make a pretty good team. Maybe we can use you again sometime. Whaddaya say?"

Bruce and Davy looked sternly at each other, then burst out laughing and gave each other a high five.

"Freeze frame! Then the closing credits roll by while I sing 'Daydream Believer.' So what do you think?"

"Hahahhaa...I'm sorry, Davy but it's too...outlandish. Too unrealistic! It was fun to listen to but it would never sell. I mean, come on. It's more like a cartoon than a real show!"

With that, Davy Jones gathered up the pages of his proposal and headed for the office door, crestfallen.

"Well, thanks for listening at least." Before he stepped out, he turned and asked, "You wouldn't happen to have the phone number of Hanna-Barbera handy would you?"

The End